Also by Colin Beazley

One Day in June

Cries from the Frozen North

The Doon Trilogy

Voices

A Tale of Two Elephants

Journeys of the Mind

Last Laugh

Silly and not so Silly Verse

The Remarkable Rise of Eric

DARK
ISLE

Colin J. Beazley

Four Boys Books

MARISCO TAVERN & St HELEN'S CHURCH

ATLANTIC OCEAN

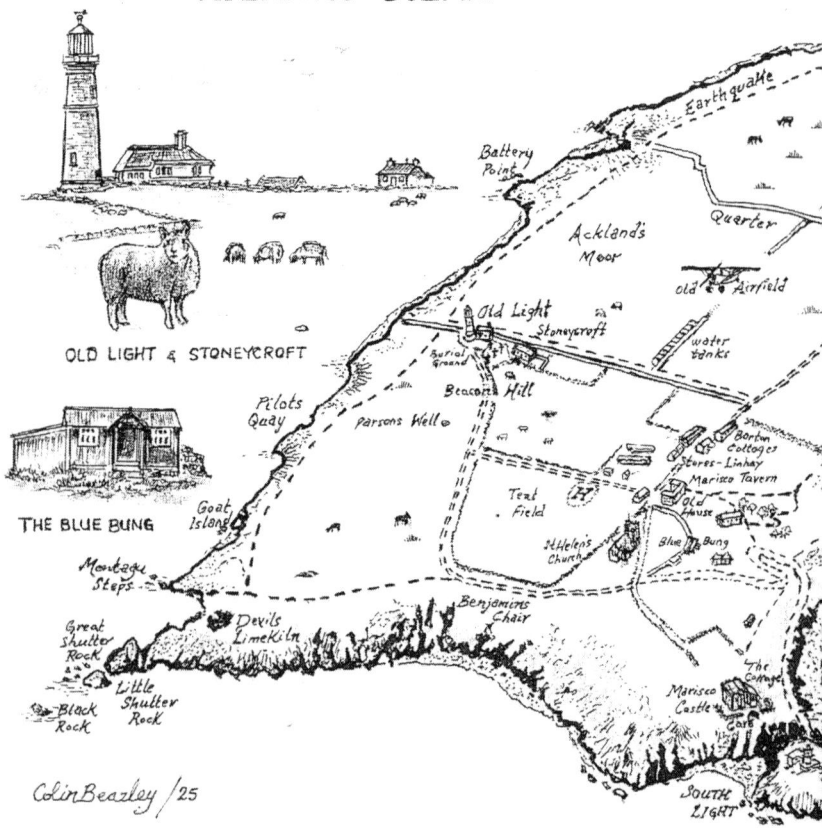

OLD LIGHT & STONEYCROFT

THE BLUE BUNG

Battery Point

Ackland's Moor

Quarter

old Airfield

Old Light

Stoneycroft

water tanks

Burial Ground

Beacons Hill

Parsons Well

Pilots Quay

Borton Cottages

Stores-Linhay

Marisco Tavern

Old House

Tent Field

St Helens Church

Blue Bung

Goat Island

Montagu Steps

Great Shutter Rock

Devils Limekiln

Benjamins Chair

Black Rock

Little Shutter Rock

Marisco Castle

The Cottage

Café

SOUTH LIGHT

ColinBeazley /25

LUNDY

NORTH LIGHT

H.

Gannet's Bay

Devils Slide

Jenny's Cove

Threequarters Wall

Tibbett's

Halfway Wall

Poundsbury

Quarry

Hospital

att

Castle Cottage

CASTLE COTTAGE

BRISTOL CHANNEL

Landing Bay

Rat Island

Mouse Island

Hells Gates

SURF POINT

Devils Kitchen

Needle's Eye

M.S. OLDENBURG · RAT ISLAND · HELL'S GATES

0   500 Metres
0   500 Yards

First published in Great Britain in 2025

Copyright © Colin Beazley 2024

The moral right of Colin Beazley to be identified as the author of this work has been asserted in accordance with the Copyright, Design and Patents Act, 1988

British Library Cataloguing-in-Publication Data
A CIP record for this title is available from the British Library

ISBN 978-1-9997457-8-3

Published by
Four Boys Books
Midhurst
Grenofen
Tavistock
Devon
PL19 9EW

Resemblance to actual people living or dead, incidents or events is purely coincidental.
This is a work of fiction.

DARK
ISLE

ONE
Lundy Island 2002

Adrift in the savage ocean, the island rose like a sinister lonely soul. The monstrous colossus of rock stood battered by the unforgiving, thunderous sea, groaning winds and driving rain assaulting any vestiges of life.

A naked man lay crumpled and broken upon an outcrop of jagged granite; any last semblance of existence had been stolen by the ceaseless surge and ebb of the freezing tide. Cries, that his restless spirit might now make, were drowned by the noise of beach stones being dragged back and forth by the relentless sea.

Yet he was not alone. A solitary fat herring gull stood upright, perched on the man's head. Its fierce yellow hooked bill hovered threateningly over his only remaining eye. The evil bird wailed, outstretched its broad grey wings, rose up, and with a hellish force, thrust its entire beak stabbing into the man's eye socket. Each lancing revealed fatty fluid and stringy twisted sinews, entangled with pale moist flesh. This only encouraged the creature to persist as it moved uneasily, shifting its clawed feet to

1

secure a better angle of attack. Half a dozen times it tore, ripping the eyelid, penetrating the waiting eyeball and optic nerve. A ring of brilliant red glowed about the bird's eyes as it picked at the ligaments, muscles and veins. Now only holes suggested where the man's eyes had once been.

Two menacing great black-backed gulls effortlessly hung high overhead, watchful; their curved wings harnessing lift from the onshore wind. Wild tongues of whipped white water crashed against the rocks below before being driven skyward, where evaporating, they fell back into the sea. Again, and again the waves came, pounding the land, smashing against the immoveable black rocks; endlessly rolling, pitching and battering the island, the only hindrance to nature's elemental power and the sea's onward journey.

Never again would this man's heart be heard, his fight had been lost, ended forever. Hypothermia alone would have been enough to bring about his untimely end, but some other force had already seen to that. It was no longer possible to look into his eyes and glance his soul, a poor, unfortunate lost soul.

At Lundy's eastern extremity, Hell's Gates was squeezed between Needle's Eye and Rat Island. Its rocky foreshore was largely out of sight from the Landing Jetty and screened from above by a rugged overhanging cliff. Of the nineteen islanders who occupied themselves with island life, or the handful of foolhardy travellers who visited at such wild and unpredictable times, few ventured to Hell's Gates. Here the body could remain a secret, undiscovered, waiting for some time.

Yet this would not be the only secret the island held.

TWO

Detective Constable Cranford Cliff had been in the force some thirty odd years. Now, on the brink of retirement, his sole aim was for an uncomplicated, painless last few months. Unsurprisingly, this also was the fervent wish of his fellow officers at Bideford Nick, for Cliff, as he was known, proved a difficult sod at the best of times. In anyone's book he was arrogant, self-opinionated, stubborn and, even on the few good days, annoying. Cliff's life had been mired with reoccurring incidents of drunkenness and periods of dark depression, largely triggered by his acrimonious marriage break-up three years earlier. This old school slob had grown cynical, jaded and lazy, avoiding anything that spelt agro or paperwork. He thought his ruse of taking time off without official leave had gone largely unnoticed and, if only he could swing it for a bit longer, life would be marginally bearable. Alas he'd overworked it to the point that his Gov'ner's compassion had long run out.

Being a North London lad, Cliff's twenty-seven years in the Met had been colourful. He'd relished dealing with the more violent end of society; reckless armed robbers, gangland heavies, GBH practitioners and out and out murderers. Broken bloody noses in the Holloway Road hostelries were not something with which he concerned himself. Cliff hadn't been great with bureaucracy and he was not averse to bending the rules, providing it got the job done. Any promotion would have necessitated exams, interview panels as well as recommendations from his immediate superiors; without doubt a step too far for Cliff. Over the years, his unorthodox approach had gained him recognition from his colleagues as being the most successful copper in the manor for convictions. Consequently, he found it unbelievable that, having gained such a track record in fighting big city crime, he had been dealt such a shitty hand and banished to this dead and alive hole in North Devon. In truth, much of his life was a mess, so why he should have expected anything different now is an utter mystery. If asked what kept him going, he would have struggled to come up with a hardly credible response; in all honesty, he hadn't got a clue. Very occasionally he wondered if he'd still got it in him, the discipline, dedication, energy and the passion for the job, or had he just grown old and tired?

Disturbing Cliff's negligible chain of thought, Sarge tossed a file onto the desk in front of Cliff's lifeless form. Cliff sighed deeply, slid the expense claim he had been doctoring to one side, lifted his foot off the wicker bin and gradually eased himself upright in his swivel chair. The chair's brown leather almost seemed to moan as it moulded itself to Cliff's rearranged body.

He uttered with exasperation, 'So what's this Sarge?'

Charlie Harris looked down at him through his tortoiseshell glasses with an obvious degree of glee.

'It's a case, and as you may remember, cases need investigating.'

Cliff gave a sigh. 'So why me?' he pressed, hardly glancing at the file.

'Well, my old son, because unlike the rest of us, you're not busy, you're not investigating anything, not even a lost puppy; am I right?'

Cliff wriggled in discomfort. This was hardly proving to be just another day at the office. He had been at a loose end sincerely hoping no one else had noticed, hope however, was clearly not enough.

'So, what have you in mind Charlie?'

'I can't cover for you anymore Cliff. The top brass seems to think you were a good detective but…'

'Ruddy right,' Cliff interjected.

Charlie added an indefatigable 'Once.'

'Hmm,' Cliff struggled, reflecting for a moment. 'So much as I find this conversation scintillating, tell me, is it a stolen handbag, a pub brawl or maybe, perish the thought, a lost puppy?'

Cliff laughed aloud.

It is said that one rarely succeeds in anything unless you have fun in what you do. Cliff couldn't remember the last time he had fun. Charlie found Cliff's attitude irritating when he was in one of these loathsome moods. He straightened and even Cliff noticed a seriousness revealed in Charlie's face.

'No, it's a body.'

Cliff, controlling his surprise, exclaimed in a hoarse voice, 'We rarely get bodies, well not unless there's an accident on the new Link Road. What do you mean body? A suicide?'

It had been an unremarkable year for Bideford Police Station. Of course, they had been kind of busy with all the usual traffic offences, petty thefts, domestics and drunken brawls in the town, nothing out of the ordinary though. Rarely is there more than one homicide a year in these parts of Devon and that's usually a domestic or suicide, but this development had the scope to change all that.

Charlie shrugged, 'Don't know, but by all accounts, it's well and truly dead.'

Cliff found the news intriguing but decided to keep that to himself.

Charlie piped up, 'You're right, we don't get that many bodies around here but this one is even more unusual, it has all the makings of a murder,' and with that he rubbed his hands together in expectation. Charlie further contemplated that the removal of an embarrassment like Cliff from the station, albeit temporarily, was most welcome. This would be bound to result in a more productive working environment.

'The gaffer wants to see you both.' a PC interrupted.

Cliff had hoped his next meeting with the Inspector would be to discuss his retirement but he wasn't naïve enough to hold onto that idea now.

'Sit yourselves down. Charlie, you've briefed Detective Cliff?'

Edwin Putt wasted no time looking for confirmation.

'Well let's get on with it. Cranford, how long were you working your last case and what was the outcome?' Cliff's mind was in a swim. 'No matter; we want you to get over there like yesterday, it's an odd one to be sure. We need you to spread an air of competence and get to grips with the investigation. It's imperative we put this one to bed pretty damn quick, time is of the essence and I want not a word to get out until we're ready to go public. The last thing we need is the press boys sniffing around. If they get their teeth into it, we'll never hear the last; they'll be coming up with all sorts of blown-up theories and they'd love a murderer or serial killer loose on a remote West Country island.'

At the mention of a 'remote West Country island' Cliff gave a dazed half-ways glance towards Charlie.

'Is that clear boys?' Edwin continued, 'Good. Do you understand the gravity of this, detective?'

'Well, to be honest Sir, until an hour ago I thought I'd be discussing my retire……..'

Charlie, jerking Cliff back to reality cut him short mid-sentence, 'I'm sure he does Sir.'

This was the kind of case Cliff needed like a hole in the head and he feared it wasn't going to be easy. On returning to the office Charlie spelt it out.

'You can't mess up with this one Cliff; everyone's eyes are going to be on you. Don't step out of line, don't flunk it and don't mess with me, I need to report up the line and fast. This will be your last case, don't blow it and don't

7

give me any reasons to regret my decision. There's no such thing as an honourable retirement in my books if this goes wrong.'

The significance of Charlie's words was not lost on Cliff. Thankfully Charlie's lecture was adjourned with the arrival of a young probie.

'Sir, I was told to report to you, Sir.' Charlie turned.

A bright eyed six-foot something P.C. stood kind of to attention. The lad couldn't have been more than twenty, complete with rosy cheeks, a freckled and spotty face and a short neat hair cut plus quiff which appeared to join both his gangly ears. His uniform looked crisp albeit a size too generous.

'This is Constable Beer, Cliff. I'm entrusting our new recruit to your care certain he'll be a vital asset helping sort our little problem. Beer has just graduated from the Training Centre as an Outstanding Student and demonstrated an enthusiasm which I believe you'll find both refreshing and invaluable.'

'I was the intake's Top Student,' Beer offered, 'and my photo appeared in the North Devon Journal. No one else in our family had been in the paper Sir.'

'Exactly,' Charlie addressed him, 'Constable, look and learn and think yourself lucky you've got the chance to work with an officer of such distinction.'

Cliff visibly smirked, well that's a surprise, he thought.

Charlie turned to Cliff, 'The doc's already on his way so don't let me hold you up. You'll be met by the Island's General Manager who is the senior official with overall responsibility on the island, he'll be your contact. Doreen on the front desk can make your arrangements.'

He hesitated, then with a glint in his eye, shared 'If you thought here was a dead and alive hole, wait until you get to Lundy. That's when you'll realise nothing in life is that easy.'

THREE

Hardly looking welcoming, Lundy's bulk rose sheer and bleak ahead of them, towering as if a slumbering monster some five hundred feet above the boiling sea; a sea which seemed to stretch endlessly, as did the sky. It was scarcely any wonder that this place had, in the past, been considered an inaccessible fortress. On occasions this rugged rock can seem inviting, almost idyllic, floating on a dazzling blue sea with a lure of mystery and enchantment awaiting the eager adventurers disembarking from the steamers and ships; but not this November day.

Today the island vanished as quickly as it appeared through shrouded thick mist and the torrential downpours driven by Atlantic winds. Huge waves crashed against the ship's hull, tossing up clouds of foaming sea, spray flooding its decks. Again, and again the 142 foot Oldenburg pitched, its 294 tons rolling at the mercies of the Bristol Channel's worst, as its forty year old German engines strained to thrust the vessel onward. Cliff had been warned that the two hour crossing today was going to be demanding, but nothing the crew weren't used to.

Fighting to keep upright on deck, Detective Cranford Cliff watched as a burly seaman frantically roped down a collection of plastic chairs which were mindlessly on manoeuvres. The departing deck-hand encouraged Cliff that it might be a good bit safer and drier below, but this advice hardly registered with him now as he stared out across the wild empty sea. Icy rain on a chilling stiff gust stared back at him, scouring his face.

He had sailed just once before to Lundy, then from Ilfracombe, and memories of that horrendous trip came rushing back to him. The journey down from London had been long and tedious, negotiating numerous trains and buses; not without incident. In the dark depths of a mid winter's night he reached his guest house, conveniently situated on Broad Street, overlooking the resort's neat harbour.

Coincidentally, the island's Land Agent, Ian Grant, was also staying there and after an early breakfast they, the only passengers that day, made their way along the quay to the awaiting craft. For some fifteen years this one-time North Sea trawler, the MV Lundy Gannet, had been the island's main link, ferrying in the winter, once a week, a handful of passengers and some ten tons of stores and livestock. At a mere 52 feet long, this twin masted vessel battled some of the most challenging of conditions on its 20 mile sailing to reach Lundy.

Cliff knew little then of the weather, other than it was fine in London, and was totally unaware that such things as shipping forecasts existed. On that day a forecast of winds continuing easterly force 4 to 5 had put their voyage in question, but, as luck would have it, this did not prevail and the skipper declared they would sail. Cliff couldn't help but worry this might be a regrettable decision and soon realised his foolishness in subjecting himself to such purgatory to reach little more than one square mile of isolated rock.

If the teenage Cliff had any aspirations of being an intrepid explorer, they were quickly dashed by the time they had left the harbour and reached the open sea. One of the sailors kindly familiarised him with the facts.

'It's gonna be bloody rough mate.'

That was perfectly clear in Cliff's memory, but the number of times he'd wished he was dead as he hung over the side, heaving and spewing his guts up, was fortunately now a blur. Meanwhile the seasoned agent and crew had wisely taken refuge huddled in the wheelhouse and were enjoying a brew.

After what seemed a life-time, enduring the stomach wrenching agony of the pounding sea and wind, along with the pervading smell of salt and the throbbing of the boat's smelly diesel, they finally anchored in the shelter of Lundy Bay, south east of the island. A small wooden boat came alongside to take supplies ashore as well as the two sole passengers. As Cliff clambered out onto the wheeled landing stage, the portly rower revealed that the weather was due to worsen, so he had no more than an hour and a half before the Gannet would weigh anchor.

A dense freezing sea mist seemed to accompany Cliff as he climbed the steep beach track, past the big house, and on to the top of the island where no view awaited him.

The agent had long since strode out ahead and now Cliff found himself alone, cold, wet and unsure if he could summon the resilience to spend a further two or so hours at sea. The warmth of the island's Tavern offered the only temporary respite along with a steaming hot mug of tea.

On the beach the same portly gent greeted Cliff with news of a storm brewing. In no time the little Gannet, belching putrid choking fumes, was battling the buffeting winds and angry seas again. Cliff, soaked and tasting the salt spray, hung over the side, his only comfort a lifejacket, and the feeling that the struggling old tub would indeed make it home.

PC Beer's gurgling belch brought Cliff back to the actuality of the moment.

'Beer,' murmured Cliff, 'you're looking the worst for wear. Are you okay?'

PC Beer dashed to the side rail and involuntarily offered up some of his breakfast to the waiting swell of which the wind kindly returned a helping or two.

'Not a sailor?' Cliff suggested.

The constable had appeared absolutely fine, almost convivial as they cruised the Taw Torridge Estuary, that was until they crossed the treacherous Bideford Bar with its constantly moving sand banks, and then everything changed.

'To be honest Sir, I don't feel too good. It's more than I can do to stay on my feet in this wind, what with all the rolling around; I daren't go below,' and with that he retched. The empty horizon offered no hope or end from this torment for the boy, and for the first time Cliff felt a degree of pity for the lad. Allowing him a moment to regain a measure of dignity, Cliff asked,

'What do the lads back at the Nick call you?'

The constable looked uncomfortable, remaining silent.

'You don't have to say.'

'Minesa,' he whispered.

'Miser?'

'No Sir; Minesa as in 'mine's a beer'.'

Cliff, conscious of the boy's forbearance refrained from laughter, just offering the faintest of smiles.

'I think we'll stick with just Beer if it's all the same to you?'

Beer nodded between gasps.

Cliff considered his own predicament. Now he'd accepted, with hardly an option, this inconvenient case, he warmed to the idea that the trip would prove to be a welcome break from the harrowing routine of duties back at the station. However, he quickly realised this was a mistake. Charlie hadn't lied but equally hadn't been totally honest with him. In truth he'd seen it as a far from straight forward investigation for this tired, self-righteous copper and Cliff was resigning himself to that fact.

The Oldenburg ploughed tirelessly onward, conquering the wild seas and weather, towards the bleached horizon. For a moment Beer wondered if they would ever find the isle, but eventually the great island mass loomed before them, half shrouded in cloud. The shivering air that greeted him seemed to bring with it a sense of dread and death.

FOUR

An almost sheer granite cliff sloped down several hundred feet from the sky to the Landing Beach. Here, roaring breakers crashed upon the half sunken shore to the accompaniment of rattling pebbles. The tide surged again with clouds of salt laden spray then returned, dragging the pebbles with it. From alongside the jetty the island appeared virtually lifeless but for half a dozen folk awaiting the ship's arrival. A Land Rover, its tail lights faintly glowing red, and the white lighthouse perched high on the cliff, were almost lost in the ghostly mist.

Upon disembarking the small group of fellow passengers gradually began to disperse along the beach road above the natural harbour, setting out on the long climb to the island's plateau and the heart of the village. Cliff remembered just how demanding that ascent was and concluded how much of a struggle that would be for an unfit copper. A woman stepped out of the waiting crowd and approached the pair, focussing on the individual that was not in uniform.

'Detective Cranford Cliff?'

Cliff judged forties, maybe younger and by her attire probably an office waller, someone who took a bit of pride in her appearance, even here. He nodded.

'I'm Charlotte Thomas, secretary to the Island's General Manager. Peter was urgently called away to Head Office on the mainland following the incident and asked me to meet you.' She looked about nervously before continuing.

'The doctor and his assistant have had the body removed to a secure room in the church and are keen to see you as soon as. With the severe weather forecast and the tides it couldn't be left on the rocks, but you can see the spot for yourselves tomorrow morning.'

Meanwhile an indignant young couple were arguing for a lift up to the village with the Land Rover's driver who was busy loading cargo and provisions onto the chugging vehicle. Despite being unwilling at first to accept 'no' as the answer, they reluctantly capitulated.

'Phil will run us up to the church,' Charlotte volunteered, 'stow your bags in the back and we'll be off.'

The alabaster white body laid stretched out on a plastic sheeted oak table, the body's marbled trunk glowed faintly blue from the cast of the vestry lamps. Not a shred of clothing covered the corpse's twisted and contorted form and its eyeless face was unrecognizable. The surreal and disturbing image haunted Beer, he took a step back; nothing in his training had prepared him for this. He'd assumed he would be immune to such horrors and beyond being shocked, but this wasn't just any corpse. Cliff

18

glared at the face and gouged eyes. He physically shuddered, and as he bit his lip and drew blood savoured a metallic taste. The mutilated visage imprinted deeply on his subconscious. He had seen death many times before in the city, but nothing quite so macabre, this was different. He looked at the doc. The silence of death hung heavy for a time.

'What do you know Doc?'

'The body is, as you can see, hardly decomposed, making the initial estimation of time in the sea…difficult. The process of saponification - the formation of a waxy substance, adipocere on the tissue would have arisen if the body had been immersed for a long period of time, but there are no signs of this. We know, however, that decomposition is much slower the lower the water temperature, and that salt will help preserve the body. The skin on the hands and feet is deeply wrinkled, putrefied and calloused: satisfactory fingerprints may be challenging. Particles of sand have filled his ear sockets and you can see his face has suffered major trauma, some of which, particularly his eyes are a result of unheavenly scavenging birds enjoying a free meal; this is unfortunate as we would routinely examine the membrane about the eyes.'

With that, the woman assisting the doctor shifted a dense matted mass of ragged black hair, thick with salt and blood, to more clearly reveal the extent of the facial disfigurement.

'Regarding the lacerations and injuries to the body, it would initially appear that these have been inflicted by the jagged outcrops and rocks. The significant head injuries

19

to the top and back of the skull are the only possible evidence of foul play. Consequently, I cannot at this early stage, conclusively rule out the use of a sharp object or undue force prior to entry of the body into the sea.'

'How long do you think he's been dead Doc?'

'As I said detective, decomposition is minimal and the body presents only mild bloating, caused by the production of intra-abdominal gas build-up.'

With this the doc paused and cautiously pressed the victim's stomach as if to demonstrate.

'Rigor mortis has disappeared so I'd say days, a week, at the most. I need to get the body over to the mainland and carry out the autopsy, then I'd be better able to tell you more.'

'Murder?' Cliff muttered asking too much.

'I can't say conclusively. Foam around the mouth and nostrils might suggest drowning but equally I can't at this stage rule it out. I've seen cases where it's been possible to make murders look like suicide. Although the body has no voice, he can still tell us things we don't yet know.'

Leaving the doc in no doubt Cliff said, 'It would be good if we kept this between ourselves. I don't want the top brass on my back, not so early.'

The doctor turned to his assistant and Charlotte.

'Can you guys arrange transport for us and our John Doe here. When I got the news of a body at the Devil's Kitchen, I wrongfully assumed it was at the waterfall along the north coast, west overlooking Clovelly Bay, but no, it had to be on an island. I've had some inconvenient locations before, but nothing with the same appealing other-worldly bleakness and unsociable conditions as this.'

He looked at Charlotte and, acknowledging her help said, 'notwithstanding your generous co-operation,' and smiled.

Beer piped up, 'Nor the horrendous journey' and swayed at the thought.

'Not a problem,' the doc shared while sorting his notes, 'here in less than ten minutes and couldn't have been a smoother trip. Unlike you chaps, a phone call and within the hour we can escape this realm on the helicopter back to Hartland Point.'

Cliff chipped in, 'What are you talking about?'

The doc's assistant, who largely had remained silent, joined in, 'We thought it was strange you opted for the sea crossing.'

The doc interrupted this banter. He glanced at the body and said, 'I think it's fitting…' and shared aloud a few words for the lost soul.

'I'll show you the spot first thing in the morning Cliff before we leave. Say 10ish, the tide will be right. I think that's me for today.'

Cliff spent that night in the old corrugated Sunday School hut, *The Blue Bung* perched high in an exposed spot looking out to sea. By now, the wind was making itself felt. This kind of howling wind wanted to bring disruption, and a moaning that touched every nerve with an overwhelming exasperation. The night proved to be long and disturbing; one of the worst he could ever recall.

FIVE

The following morning the group, along with Charlotte at the wheel of the Land Rover, journeyed down to the Landing Bay. Reaching the jetty, the doc looked at Cliff and said,

'How did you sleep?'

Cliff shrugged. 'You ought to take care of yourself.' The doc continued, 'We needed to move the body off the beach at Devil's Kitchen as the squawking gulls were having a field day pecking over the corpse. In the end we had to throw rocks to get them to scatter. With the scene being impossible to effectively cordon-off and situated so close to the landing jetty, we considered that once the word got out, it may have proved too much for the inquisitive islanders or visitors to ignore. We scoured the area as best we could for related debris and items, then put bags over his head and hands. Although he'd been in the sea, he may still have secrets and clues which we desperately need to discover.'

The doc led the group around behind the new wooden divers' shed onto the slippery outcrops, the loose shingle, then over the jagged rocks beside the massive Rat Island to where the body had lain. The going was difficult between the rock pools, their steps sinking into seaweed strewn gullies as they began to wade the shallows. As Cliff crouched down attempting to look more closely, he stumbled, lost his balance momentarily, and stretching out to steady himself, cut his hand on a rough rock. Salt spray carried by the wind swept over them, chilling each to the bone. Water ran down Cliff's face as he tried to make himself heard.

'Someone must be missing this man, waiting for him to walk in or call. He was a son, brother, husband or father, so someone must be worried, but they won't be expecting this dreadful news that's for sure.'

'Here's a teaser for you Detective Cliff,' said the doc as he unwrapped a Mars bar and took a bite. 'If indeed a crime was committed, where was the scene of the crime; where did it all start?'

Cliff immediately responded, 'Every crime starts in the mind, but I know what you mean.'

Cliff looked up, staring at the weak blue patches between the ominous dark rain clouds in the ever-changing sky.

They hastily retired to the warmth of the Marisco Tavern, the island's hub, seeking shelter from the breaking weather. Settling down on the pub's balcony away from inquisitive ears they appraised themselves of the situation. The doc was clear, as he savoured his single malt; he couldn't come to any firm decision but was inclined to believe someone else was likely to be involved. His assistant meanwhile was totally content with her half of cider, while PC Beer downed a pint of bitter shandy as if it was some kind of competition. Cliff refrained from any alcohol and tackled a bowl of steaming broth, the ingredients of which he was uncertain. The Tavern was hardly full, a dozen or so islanders and guests were enough to ensure an atmosphere, and a buzz of chatter regarding the latest wildlife and bird sightings, or ships which had found their end on the island's shores or indeed failing that, just the impending weather. Meanwhile, Charlotte was busy seeking out Shirley, the woman who had first discovered the corpse, to arrange for her to meet up with Cliff later that afternoon.

Seizing the opportunity, Cliff briefed his young and inexperienced rookie. 'We've got to get on top of this Beer, and quick. We need results. Firstly, get hold of the Coast Guard and look into local shipping movements – commercial, passenger, fishing and pleasure craft in the vicinity, say for the past month. Also determine the sea's movements, tides and currents, so we can get a picture of where he may have entered the water; that might help track down his clothes. Finding those would undoubtedly help us identify the body. Patterns of the wind direction and force, combined with the weight and buoyancy of the body will also have a bearing; see what you can find. You need to become a bit of a part time oceanographer Beer. Perhaps we can organise a search of the island and accessible coastline. Leave that one with me, I'll talk to Charlotte.'

'This is turning out to be quite an adventure Sir.'

As soon as Beer had opened his mouth, he knew he'd made a mistake. Hardly content he added, 'When will the team arrive Sir?'

'You're looking at 'The Team' Beer. There are over 1000 unidentified bodies found in the UK each year, and I have no intention that this will remain just another mysterious statistic let me tell you. I've no desire to attend a funeral for an unknown man.'

Even the naive Beer knew when he'd been put in his place and the horrific memory of the body came flooding back to him.

After a moment he said, 'Well Sir, at 6 foot 6 inches he is one… was one, of only 1% of the population.'

Dismissing the comment, Cliff said, 'We must establish if someone on the island knew the man or anything about what happened. What's the link between him and Lundy? There must be one. And why did he end up here? We need to look further afield - The Regional and National Missing Persons Registers - get the station to check them out for anything relevant and maybe Interpol's 'Black Notice', but we may need to come to that one later.'

This investigation, Cliff realised, was clearly going to push boundaries beyond which Beer was familiar.

Cliff impressed upon him, 'Remember, this is not a job, it's a calling which we do, not for the miserly wage and poor conditions, but because we want to solve a crime and stop a criminal.'

Cliff even surprised himself with his words. He had once been regarded as an annoying perfectionist, never still, always on the go, to the point of being irritatingly exhausting to be near. He was now endeavouring to mould Beer in the self-same way.

'We'll meet up here at the end of the day, say four. I'll have seen the witness who discovered the body and will chat with Charlotte about organising a search of the island and interviewing folk. You can update me on what you found out.'

The clatter of a typewriter greeted Cliff as he entered the cosy Island Office. He was amazed to see Charlotte working away at the keys and not on a computer. She was well used to people's surprise and explained that this way she was not bothered by power problems.

'Shirley's on her way,' Charlotte said and, as if on cue, she arrived at the door flushed, having rushed to avoid the downpour. Cliff could sense the earthy smell of the rain as the woman entered. He had given some consideration to his line of questioning but as it turned out he need not have bothered.

'Shirley, this is Detective Cranford Cliff, he wants to ask you a few questions about….'

'The body, Charlotte,' the wispy woman interrupted.

'Cliff, this is Shirley Brückner, she is one of our faithful having been on the island for, eight years isn't it, Shirley?'

'Nine next month Charlotte.'

'Is that right Shirley. And how do you spend your time here?' Cliff asked.

It was as if she had been invited to stage her one woman show.

'Firstly, there's my work in the Tavern, part time of course, but I'm vital in ensuring an appetising and tasty range of dishes are on the menu. I love baking and being a great cook, even if I say it myself, means it's easy to keep the kitchen running smoothly. Have you eaten there yet? Oh, I don't expect so, you've only just arrived, haven't you?

'Then there's the cleaning. I help with the visitor change-overs in the houses and cottages, that's obviously busier in season. In spring I get involved with the island flocks of Texel and Cheviot sheep, and the Soays, they originate from St Kilda and the Faroes you know? That's a fun time, we all pitch in as they more or less have freedom over the entire 1000 acres, so there's lots of walking. And of course, I have my regular class. Well, it's a group really, there's four of us and we get together to research the island's history. It's steeped in ancient folklore along with a mystical past going back to the dawn of time. It was once home to the Vikings, pirates and convicts and called the *'Kingdom of Heaven'* you know. Amazing, isn't it?'

Cliff realised that this was a woman who found it hard to stop talking and wondered if the recent 'murder' made the island even more amazing. He was now about to ask her what happened, hopeful that it would not be what she imagined happened.

'A Lundy resident called through to Bideford Police Station at 8.48 am on the 29th last month reporting the discovery of a body on Devil's Kitchens beach near Hell's Gates. The duty officer took down the information but the caller withheld their name. Sceptical, the officer sought confirmation by ringing the Island Office and was told that a cook at the Tavern had just come into the office confirming her sighting. Did you make that call to the Police Station, Shirley?'

'Yes. Do you know the phone must have rung a dozen or more times before it was answered.'

'Right. And did you report the sighting to the office here?'

Shirley nodded.

'Good,' Cliff confirmed, 'tell me exactly what happened and what you saw?'

'I simply saw the body, as I said.'

'There is nothing simple about seeing a body. Why were you there Shirley?'

She looked to Charlotte who had remained silent, then she wriggled in the chair before continuing.

'Well, every morning at seven-thirty regardless of the weather, I take Max, my retriever, for our morning walk. That day we went down to the jetty. I don't know why but we just did. As I neared the little bay, I saw someone on the rocks. Now I know they do snorkelling down there, not this early in the year though. It looked like somebody sunbathing, yet it wasn't sunny. I called out but they didn't move. Max was getting restless, barking at the pesky gulls, wanting to move on, sniffing around the cave entrance, but I thought I would take a closer look. I saw they were naked. I also noticed the face and the blood. Well, that was enough for me I can tell you.'

'What did you think when you saw the body?'

'What do you mean?'

'What did you think had happened?'

'To be honest I thought they'd been murdered.'

'Why?'

'We don't get people falling into the sea here. It was such a dreadful sight you know; I'll never forget it.' She paused. 'Lundy is known as 'the other world', and the Celts believed it was one of the 'islands of the dead.' I believe it's a gateway to the gods, a thin place of isolation that brings us closer to the divine, a connection.'

Cliff felt Shirley's demeanour had changed, he couldn't exactly explain how, but she was certainly different. There was almost something altogether sinister in her words.

'Thanks Shirley, your account is a great help. If I need to clarify anything, will it be okay to speak again?'

Shirley looked anxious.

Cliff said, 'I now need a quick word with Charlotte, thanks again.' With that, he escorted Shirley to the door and the awaiting rain.

Charlotte looked at Cliff, 'She's a good soul, a bit on the folklore side, but that's not unusual for islanders.'

'No, that was useful and I believed her every word. Charlotte, what's the possibility we could somehow search the island's coast?'

'Where? We've tall cliffs to the south and west, with heavily overgrown thickets and steep hanging valleys on the east facing the mainland. It's eight miles round you know.'

'Ideally, all of it!'

'Looking for what?'

'Clothes and anything unusual?'

She considered for a moment. 'There are three or four energetic islanders who regularly walk the island, some leading tourist rambles in the season. I am sure they would be willing to help. If I got them together, are you happy to brief them?'

'Of course,' Cliff said.

'Oh, I've assumed you'll want to interview all the islanders and the few visitors, including me. So, I'll draft a schedule for the next two or three days around their working and stop-overs. Is that okay?'

Cliff couldn't fail but to be impressed by her clear and uncomplicated air. They chatted on together about the island, the sea and her.

'How did it go Beer?' Cliff's words brought the constable up with a jolt as they entered the Tavern.

'Oh, fine Sir.'

They moved to a quiet corner of the bar. 'I finally got through to the station on the pay phone and, having fed it with all my loose change, told them what we needed. Doreen confirmed back to me our requests and said she'd get right onto it, then put me through to Jack in CID, and he's going to look into Missing Persons. I emphasised to them both that it might seem a crazy load of information but that we needed answers urgently as we're dealing with a dead body. They know, Sir, that at present, the enquiries must be handled sensitively and in confidence.'

Beer sat back in his chair, content.

'They're faxing anything they've got.'

Cliff was impressed. 'Well done, Beer, it sounds as if you're getting to grips with it.'

'And Sir, Tracey said they're leaving tomorrow.'

'Tracey?' Cliff couldn't help but smile.

'Yes Sir, the doc's assistant; they and the body are being airlifted by chopper to the District Hospital in Barnstaple. How did it go with you Sir? Any revelations?'

'Fine. They're a strange bunch, well some are. The woman who discovered the body, apart from being fixated with Lundy being a gateway to another world, was quite clear about what happened and, in truth, I tend to believe her. Charlotte's organising an interview schedule for us with the folk on the island and arranging a group to check out the coast line. She's certainly efficient.'

It was Beer's turn to smile.

'What's up Beer?'

'Nothing Sir. Something odd did happen just before you arrived. I was approached by a young man who wanted to know what we knew about the body. He was most insistent. I told him there was nothing I could tell him and although I pressed him, he wouldn't explain why and who he was. Although others saw him, no one recognised the youth.'

'Shit,' Cliff exclaimed.

'He looked ordinary, but…. Well, I thought even the press can look ordinary.'

'Exactly Beer, and even a murderer can look ordinary, they can look like anybody, just like you and me.'

Cliff's update with the Gov'ner was brief and to the point.

'I'll keep it short Charlie, the land-line is temperamental. The doc tells me he's considered accidental death, suicide and….'

'Suicide would be straightforward and means we'd be able to close the case quickly,' Charlie intervened.

'We can't yet jump the gun, Sir, we need the pathologist's detailed report after the autopsy. At this moment, the cause of death is still unknown and he can't rule out anything but cautions us that we should, at this stage, not ignore murder.'

Charlie sounded depressed with the idea.

'I don't recall there ever being a murder on Lundy, not since the pirates, and it's the last thing we need now.'

'Well Sir, I don't think that's our choice.'

'Tell me, how's the investigation going Cliff? We've urgently got to find out who he is, before the Press get hold of it and tell the world, making us look like fools. Your approach in the past has, at times, been unorthodox to say the very least, but I've got to admit you get results.'

'Identification may not be that easy Sir. His face is in a right old mess, while his hands, and specifically fingers, have seen significant damage from being in the sea. With no clothes or documents we may struggle. We'll need to explore dental records, and maybe state-of-the-art DNA comparison. My experience of the island is like stepping back in time, it's clearly a unique place. We're forced to believe what they tell us, that is until someone speaks out, because the island's not blessed with a single CCTV camera.'

'This has the potential of turning into a bloody mess, you need to stay on top of this one Cliff.'

SIX

By the time Cliff reached the corrugated iron hut, he was completely drenched. Shaking off the worst of the rain, he brushed his wet hair back from his face as he entered. Distant thunder grumbled, along with the darkening of the sky, as a brutal sea wind tore against the island and the hut. With the throw of a switch a single light bulb, hanging on a twisted flex wire from the centre of the room's ceiling, dimly glowed. The accommodation appeared tired, a memorial to a time forgotten. Peeling wallpaper, drab paintwork and a layer of dust told of a neglected existence. A rustic pot belly stove decorated the room's corner but no fuel was evident. He sat on the bed, its frame creaking, announcing his presence. The lumpy blue and white striped mattress immediately declared the existence of numerous previous bed-fellows; agitated, he accepted that this was to be his home for the next few days. Slumping back on the bed the steel bedframe echoed its displeasure as, shattered, he tried to sleep.

An ill-fitting window rattled violently, its frame groaning from the wind sweeping across the headland, ripping and threatening all in its path. Nothing could escape it. And with it came the black, when everything seems to change and a sense of dread descends. As the relentless rain beat down on the tin roof, the hut had become a very different and inhospitable place. He fought hard to try and sleep but it was impossible, the noise of the buffeting storm was too much. Pulling the pillows over his head, he tried to dull the tumult, but to no avail, the storm was so loud it overwhelmed everything. He stripped the bed and attempted to prop the mattress up against the window, then laid curled on the bed with only the blankets. Nothing worked, nothing stopped the infernal racket. He lay awake feeling as though he was being slowly squeezed by some dreadful force until he could hardly breathe. Tormented, he agonised how anyone could sleep in this horrendous bloody gale. The fury had not come alone; when exhaustion finally overcame him, so did a frightful dream.

Freezing, he could feel himself slipping closer to the cliff's edge. The man's hand clasped his, a clasp of hope, begging to be saved. Cliff sensed exhaustion spread throughout his body, his grip loosened as he became completely swamped with fatigue. He could feel the man's hand shaking as they slid ever closer to the brink. The man screamed, yet no-one else heard his cries.

Cliff stared into the man's eyes whose look of deep despair transfixed and haunted him. Not a word was said. Something weighty came down and struck the man about his head, someone else was there. The force of the blow threw the man off balance and his contorted body fell over the sheer edge and plunged into the depths of the ocean below, disappearing forever. Cliff felt panic grip and overwhelm him.

Cliff woke with a start. He exhaled deeply. After a few moments he swung his legs to the side of the bed and down to the floor. Leaning forward he cupped his face in his palms and remained like that, silent and still, frozen in time, utterly drained.

'You'll be sorry when I'm gone,' he said aloud to no-one as he looked at himself in the shower room mirror. He saw a face that he didn't recognise, one that belonged to someone else.

The first rays of the day cut through the morning's early mist as the shimmering sun pushed its way through the clouds. Cliff lifted the mattress from the window and as he did, a silvery light bathed the room in an unreal glow. Making his way up the muddy track to the village the shrill cry of the gulls, wheeling high and wide above, troubled him. He felt anything but 'normal' for the horror of the night still filled his head.

SEVEN

Lundy awoke slowly, so slowly one might wonder if it would be anything other than a sleepy day.

Cliff deliberated; there was a crime to solve and despite being deprived of sleep it was crucial he stayed focussed. He had a job to do and needed to cope with the many thoughts that were swirling and colliding in his weary head.

'How are you sleeping?' Beer's words greeted Cliff who was engrossed checking his watch.

'I'm not. It's the ruddy wind; the noise is endless. Never mind me, what about you?'

'Not too bad, I'm in the Old House in the village with some other visitors. It's warm, friendlyish and quiet there. We have to share a loo though, but it's okay.'

'Let's grab a coffee,' Cliff proposed, his first for the day. With a piping hot coffee and tasty roll from the Tavern's kitchen they joined Charlotte in her office.

'I thought it would make sense to arrange the interviews in here.' Charlotte looked for approval, Cliff shrugged with indifference.

'Fine.'

'There are few visitors on the island so you shouldn't be disturbed; I'll post a sign on the door saying it's closed apart from the interviews.' Charlotte continued in a different vein.

'Having spoken with PC Beer, I thought it might be better Cliff, if you move to Castle Cottage. It's built on the outside of the Castle Keep and much more sheltered than the Old School. It will also offer you more space to use as your base, plus it's got a great view and will be quieter.'

Cliff was somewhat thrown, when on earth did Beer have that chat with Charlotte? He contemplated that maybe she was a bit of a mind reader.

Cliff had a degree of apprehension as to how the day would pan out. It was one thing to undertake house-to-house enquiries, strolling the local urban pavements, rattling the door knockers, but quite a different job here on Lundy. To start with, how would this tight community take to a rank outsider, a copper at that, being dropped into the middle of their world in which confiding with others doesn't come as second nature? And also, they don't have any door knockers here! He proceeded to brief Beer.

'The first lesson is that the truth is open to interpretation. It's dependent on the situation of who's sharing the so-called truth. Some carefully choose their words to confuse and mislead the listener, they lie. You see there's a world of difference between what we believe is true, wish is true and what is true. Where truth ends, so often fantasy begins; so take care, what is said may not be gospel.

'A good copper will be rigorous in spotting clues, inconsistencies, and shrewd in sniffing out liars. Everyone has secrets. Some that don't matter and others, that if revealed, change everything. We need to get beneath the obvious. There are so many ways a criminal can trip up, unwillingly leaving countless clues. All we've got to do is make it happen. If the clues are there, we've got to find them. People commit crimes for a whole lot of different reasons and that's what we've got to uncover. The behaviour of a guilty person isn't always reflected in their personality. It's essential we see them as they are, not as they want to be seen. Many will hide in broad daylight, amongst the shadows, playing a game, half yearning to be discovered.

'There's no room for sloppy detective work Beer, we need our wits about us because seeking the truth can be dangerous. Stay on your toes; I don't know how they'll take to us 'strangers' but I guess we'll soon find out.'

Throughout Charlotte had busied herself in the outer office. A rap came on the office door, it opened and in struggled a wheezing, over-weight middle aged man. The stocky guy looked blindly about until he glimpsed Charlotte,

'Roy, this is Detective Cranford Cliff and PC Beer, the ones I was telling you about. They want to ask you a few questions.' Roy appeared to ease somewhat.

'Shall I sit?' he asked, clearly needing to recover from his exertion, 'only I'm a bit late because I lost track of the time.' He lowered himself into a chair.

'I'm off now Roy, I've work to do, you'll be okay?' Charlotte encouraged.

Roy half smiled as he gave the two the once over.

Cliff kicked-off. 'Thanks for coming Roy, we wanted to have a chat. Tell us something about what you get up to here on the island? What do you do? Take your time Roy, there's no rush.'

'Oh right,' he blustered wiping his forehead with a large oily handkerchief, 'well I'm the resident engineer, one of 'em anyway. I look after the power and water on the island, help to that is. You probably heard about our own electricity Aerogenerator on top of the island; that was my baby. You won't have seen her, she's been long gone. So, the gennies are my responsibility now along with the pumping systems on our reservoirs: it's an important job you know.'

'I can imagine, you keep the island's pulse beating,' Cliff coaxed.

'I heard something had happened but I was surprised to hear you chaps were over here.'

'Do you know what happened?' Beer tried.

'No, what? I tend to keep myself to myself.'

'We've found a body.'

Much to the boy's astonishment Roy replied, 'I'm not surprised.'

'Really?' Cliff pressed.

'Yerr. I'm coming across bones all the time when I'm digging in cables and pipes, some are sheep and goats but

42

a lot are human. The island's lousy with 'em. Lundy used to be the hang out for the pirate Captain Kidd, you know? All sorts of things went on here.'

Cliff attempted to bring him back to reality.

'We found this man's body on the rocks.'

'I heard something cropped up but didn't know what. Bugger me!'

'Have you been aware of any strangers, a tall man on the island recently, perhaps in the past weeks? Maybe someone acting unusually?'

'I can't say I have, but there again, I tend to work in the back of beyond.'

Cliff thanked Roy and impressed upon him to let them know if anything came to mind.

'What do you think, Sir?'

'At the very least a 16 stoner, who having abused his body for too long is now suffering the consequences.'

'What do you think Beer, and let's drop the 'sir' for 'Boss.'

'I don't think he knows anything useful about it, Boss.'

'I've got to admit I agree with you. Who's next?'

Beer referred to Charlotte's notes. 'Marion, who works with Shirley in the kitchen'

'This is going to be interesting,' Cliff suggested sarcastically.

Marion shuffled in on the dot. A sturdy woman sporting coarse features; a chubby wrinkled face, rotund physique and revealing short plump legs as she slumped clumsily down in the chair.

Cliff could have sworn she looked a bit flat footed but who was he, a copper, to be the judge of that?

'We're here to discover what we can about the body.' Cliff knew there was no need to beat around the bush, after all she worked with Shirley.

'It's a rum job to be sure, but there again, who knows what's gone on on our little island in the past.'

'Do you know anything about it?' Cliff said.

'No officer, only what Shirley told me, and I guess told you. I've no idea who he is, he's not one of us islanders.'

'Have you noticed any strangers recently, visitors in the Tavern, folk who are not still around but you don't think have left for the mainland?' Beer persisted.

'Have you any idea Marion, who he was?' Cliff tried.

'No, we don't get many visitors this time of year, just a handful.'

'Is there anything else you want to say Marion?'

'Yes. This is my spiritual home, a home where I belong and have no intention of leaving. Don't go spoiling it for us.' And with that she went as quickly as her legs would carry her.

Nigel Routh was a totally different kettle of fish. A tall wiry individual with a distinctive weathered face, possessing a fine bone structure punctuated by receding wispy silver hair. All in all, a fit fifties-something man who had called Lundy his home for the past twenty-two years.

'I get involved in the 'Rockpool Rambles' to the Devil's Kitchen, behind Rat Island with the Field Studies Group, but not at this time of year. It's a super place for exploring the seashore with the pools and gullies bursting with marine life. There's a whole variety of seaweeds, anemones and corals, as well as barnacles, limpets and of course crabs and fish. With warming, the seagrass meadows, seaweeds and kelp forests are becoming increasingly important. Do you know, our oceans are warming at a rate of about 0.15°c every decade, well something like that. And here on the island we've experienced a massive decline in seabirds, our puffins are close to extinction. I hope the steps we are taking, along with our voluntary marine nature reserve, will help check that.' He took a breath, the boys waited, quite enjoying the lecture.

'The Devil's Kitchen, isn't that where you found the body?'

Cliff perked-up, 'What do you know about it?'

Nigel considered for a moment, 'Not a lot, but you understand my work, looking after the wildlife and livestock, means I get around and I'll often walk the island late at night. A week or so back, I stumbled upon a lonely soul striding out late at night. He hardly acknowledged my greeting and quickly took off. I've never seen him before or since and because of the overcast night, would struggle to describe him. His gait and arched back led me to believe he wasn't young, and his awkwardness that he wasn't used to this terrain. As we passed, I couldn't help but think how tall he was, taller than my six feet.'

Cliff and Beer looked at one another.

'Whereabouts was this, Nigel? Your encounter?' Cliff waited.

'To be honest, I didn't give it another thought, until now that is. You see I occasionally spend a night in the Lantern room of the defunct Old Light standing on Beacon Hill, the highest place on the island. At 96 feet high, overlooking the whole of the island, the views at night can be magical. That particular night I was west of the Lighthouse Field, just north of Parsons Well, heading for the Light when he passed. He was bearing south, perhaps towards the village or maybe St Helen's. I don't know if that's helpful?'

'Very much so,' Cliff acknowledged, 'if there's anything else you remember contact us immediately, as things stand, we'll be here for a while. Any chance you can recall the date and time?'

Nigel looked uncertain.

'Let us know. I'm certain we'll want to speak again,' and with a shake of hand, Beer ushered him out.

'Result!' he said.

'The odds are moving in our favour with that *slipper and newspaper man!*' Cliff speculated with a degree of relief.

Shirley entered. 'I've been waiting for Nigel to go.'

'Thanks Shirley, we were purely wondering if there was anything you wanted to add?' Beer was getting in his stride.

The woman appeared flustered, 'No not really.'

'What do you mean, 'not really' Shirley?' Cliff was intent to pursue his line of questioning.

'You'd be wanting me to betray folk.'

'No,' Cliff came straight back, 'you'd not be betraying them, you'd be saving them.'

'We're not used to this kind of stuff here.'

'Sure. Let me try to explain. You work in the kitchen Shirley, so you'll appreciate when I say that the only way I can get to the heart of the matter is to carefully peel back the layers one by one; a bit like peeling an onion. Do you understand?'

She looked pensive. 'You might want to talk to Francesca.'

'Francesca?' Cliff said.

She was determined not to reply, and Cliff could see that.

'Why her?' Beer implored, but Cliff cut him short and, sincerely thanking Shirley for her help, he led her to the door.

Any demoralisation for Beer quickly passed with the arrival of trim Polly and her alluring beam.

'Hi, not too early I hope?'

There was no stopping Beer. 'Absolutely not, sit yourself down. You must be…' still dazed he checked the list, 'Polly Shaw?'

She looked at him, smiled, then gave Cliff the eye. Cliff relaxed and let Beer have his head.

'What exactly do you get up to on the island?'

'Get up to?' she said and giggled.

'What do you do here?' he corrected flustered by her response.

'I work in the Tavern, serving food and behind the bar. When I'm not doing that, they have me cleaning. I never wanted to stay at home, but here I am stuck on this island, sometimes it feels like a prison. If I had wanted a digital detox I wouldn't have come here.'

Cliff could see Beer was starting to lose it.

'I'm Detective Cliff; I can see it must be rough at times for a young lass like yourself, but I can assure you that this is nothing like a prison. It could be a lot worse; maybe you need to perfect some escape methods, there's a hundred and one things you can do with butter you know.'

She nervously brushed her blonde hair back from her face and ignoring Cliff asked, 'Does his superior manner come with training?'

Beer jumped in without thinking, 'No it comes naturally' and instantly regretted his words.

Cliff laughed out loud much to the relief of Beer.

Cliff fixed on her, 'Do you know anything about our body Polly, or the stranger?' She fidgeted and after a respectable pause admitted, 'No.'

As Cliff opened the door, he generously suggested she practised her escape techniques.

'That was a bit harsh Boss,' Beer piped-up.

'I could have sworn I detected your pulse quickening momentarily Constable, am I right?'

Beer didn't respond.

'Mind you she was wearing sensible shoes,' Cliff said.

'We've another before lunch Boss, and it's…. Shirley's one, Francesca West!'

In Cliff's eyes here was a woman that ten years ago he could well have imagined being wildly attracted to. As far as Beer was concerned, she was a beauty well past her prime. Neither man at this stage fully appreciated exactly what they were letting themselves in for.

'Will this take long?' she said.

'It needn't, but depends on what, if anything, you have to tell us.'

Cliff instantly knew he had to be firm if they stood any chance of learning why Shirley was so keen they interviewed the woman.

Francesca began, 'Why are you so fixated on this guy?'

Cliff fielded, 'Because we've got to find out who he is, whose son he is, who's missing him, does he have a family who need to know, why was he here of all places, there's got to be a reason, did he know someone? And, of course, what happened? I'm sure you can appreciate that until we know the answers, it leaves us in a bit of a dilemma.'

She stared him down with eyes that hadn't dulled with the years, eyes that were sharp and piercing.

'Why is it that police are always men and only listen to women if they're forced to but don't really hear them, and only hear what they want to hear.'

Beer was struggling to get his head wrapped round just how aggressive she was.

'Surely it was just an accident, a stranger who wandered too close to the edge.'

'Do people come here to escape something, someone or somewhere, to find something they haven't got? Why did you come here Francesca?' Cliff could hardly have been more direct.

'I'm an artist, I came in search of a land full of drama and intrigue, a place of solitude and emotions, and I found it.'

Cliff judged that the interview needed a redirection.

'What do you paint, landscapes? And what media do you favour? My mother was a well-respected portrait artist in north London, back in the seventies.'

'I adore capturing the idyllic, untameable barren landscape of Lundy through the seasons, and the ever-changing weather that the Atlantic has in store. This place is steeped in history; legends where facts become blurred with myth. Imagine a land inhabited by wolves in sheep's clothing. Sheep whose hearts ran with the blood of others, racing across this land to an uncertain future.'

There was a silence before she spoke again, 'Forgive me, I am just a meandering old fool.'

Cliff knew full well it was dark moments like these that can tell you so much.

'I'll be frank with you Francesca, I don't think you're in anyway involved but someone is and, maybe you, along with everyone else on this island, can help us. If anything comes to mind, anything at all, no matter how trivial it may seem, don't hesitate to let us know. I'm certain we'll be in touch before long, thanks for your co-operation, it's been invaluable.'

She looked ponderously on and then as if an after thought said, 'It's hard to imagine what drowning is like unless you've tasted it.'

'What did you make of that Boss? I'm beginning to have my doubts about the human race, and I noticed you didn't ask her directly if she knew something?'

'You're right Beer. She's an intelligent woman, someone who understands human nature. She knows what's going on; somehow, we've got to get her to tell us one way or another.'

They grabbed a bite and two strong coffees from the adjoining kitchen of the Tavern and after fifteen minutes were into the next interview.

'Jago Thomas, a local lad, mid-twenties, worked as a boatman on the quay, a driver and gardener. According to Charlotte's notes a lively character, whatever that means. Shall I get him in Boss?'

'Wheel him in Beer, let's see what we've got.'

What they had was a black, curly haired young man complete with tash and wild beard, staring at them through bright hazel eyes.

Cliff kicked-off, 'Is it okay to call you Jago?'

'That's my name, granddad.'

He took no time to make his unsettling presence felt.

'Why am I here?'

'That's a good question,' Cliff was quickly getting the measure of the lad. 'We're questioning everybody about the dead body you see, because everybody appears to have free run of the island. Then there's the fact that the body was found near Rat Island on the beach, not a stone's throw from the jetty and cove where you work. Am I right?'

'I had nothing to do with it.'

Cliff looked to Beer and asked, 'I don't think I suggested that did I, Constable?'

'No Sir, not at all.' Beer decided this was an occasion to revert to 'sir.'

'You coppers come here thinking this is the arse end of nowhere, full of a load of idiots, well it's not.'

'And the idiots?' Cliff said toying with the lad.

'Look at me you stubborn old sod of a detective, do I look like a murderer? I'm sick of this, I haven't done anything wrong.'

Seeing the lad's point Cliff suppressed his annoyance with the lad's attitude.

'I'm sorry, I think we've got off on the wrong foot.'

'Right.' Jago appeared to calm down.

'Let's have a coffee; white, any sugars?'

Jago gave him his order and Beer shot off to the kitchen. On his return the two were talking away like long lost friends.

'We've been chatting about my first visit in the tiny Lundy Gannet and the row boat landing me on the beach. Jago's been explaining that Rat Island forms one arm of the wide bay which takes in the jetty and Landing Beach, providing shelter from the Atlantic westerly winds. In the past as many as 300 ships have taken refuge at one time in the waters of Lundy Roads Bay. It seems the waters can be hazardous around the island but the bay offers a safe haven. So much so, any passing or visiting vessels will berth in these waters. Jago's not seen any cruisers or yachts about the island over the past month. He is aware, however, that there was talk of a missing passenger,' Cliff turned to Jago, 'tell the Constable what you told me.'

'When the Oldenburg offloads its passengers and supplies, we load the cargo to be shipped off island and that's the chance to catch-up with the crew. About three sailings back the purser, Frank, was anxious that one passenger hadn't turned up for the return trip, he'd booked the ride but was nowhere to be seen on departure. If my memory's right, he never did show. I think they thought it must have been a mistake by the office and assumed he was staying over. I never knew what happened in the end, but Frank will know back at Bideford Quay, Cliff.'

'We need to check that one out Beer, and Jago's kindly offered to take us round the caves near where the body was, on the off chance we might find something.'

Beer was still reeling from Jago's apparent turn around. 'Great.'

'Thanks Jago, we'll definitely get back to you on that and I'll owe you a pint.'

'I'll hold you to that Cliff.' And with that he was gone.

'Boss, what on earth did I miss?'

'I levelled with him and told him I'd handled far more difficult gits than he was trying to be, and had given every one of them an exhausting run for their money. We agreed to a truce and you saw the rest. Seriously Beer, we need more allies on the island like Jago if we're going to solve this one.'

The seemingly innocent pair of island visitors who breezed in next painted a pretty picture of youthful newly-weds. Tom, probably no more than twenty-five was lean and keen, wrapped in his blue and yellow trimmed 'Berghaus' anorak. Strapped to his back a bright red rucksack, plump with goodies, whereas Sue modelled a pathetically fluorescent orange day bag over her camouflage windcheater. They hardly looked the business as far as Cliff was concerned.

'Holiday or adventure?' he prompted.

Sue couldn't wait, 'It's our anniversary, imagine a whole year.'

Cliff couldn't, while Beer was still playing catch-up.

'You've been married a year?'

'Oh no silly, we've been going out for a year,' Sue was keen not to be misunderstood.

'So why here?' Cliff directed to the silent Tom.

'Sue thought we could do a spot of bird watching and she loves deer.'

'And we thought we'd embrace the elemental brutality of an isolated island,' Sue was away.

'You could have caught the brutality, as well as the deer on Exmoor during the rut, avoiding the sea crossing and much closer to home. Incidentally, where is home?' Cliff waited.

They looked at each other, exchanged puzzled glances and Tom added, 'Croydon.'

Beer couldn't help himself. 'Croydon? Why the hell….sorry, why here?'

'We saw it on TV and it looked so romantic,' Sue said but Tom didn't let that go.

'But that was filmed in the summer,' he said turning to Sue.

'Ah!' Cliff shared 'I sense we could chat like this for hours but what we want to know is, since you've been here have you seen or witnessed anything that's a bit odd, strange? Anything at all?'

Another exchange of glances took place between them and then Tom spoke directly to Sue, 'Shall we?'

'Yes, I think we should, it can't do any harm.'

The boys were riveted, hopeful.

'We found this when we were walking the cliff path over on the west,' Tom confessed as he started to hoick it out of his rucksack.

'I hope we won't get into trouble but it seemed too good and stupid to leave it out,' Sue explained.

Next up was Katrina, a middle-aged jolly soul who worked part-time in the Linhay General Stores and, being what Cliff took to be an athletic type, helped out with anything that needed doing. As a walker she explained she'd passed close to where the body was found about five days earlier but didn't see anything there.

Phil, who had picked them up in the Land Rover on their arrival, came across as an all round good sort but was unable to throw any light on who the stranger was.

Guy, jobbing builder and decorator, on the other hand, came across as a bit of a lazy slouch. The kind of dissatisfied individual who wheedles his way in and causes nothing but disruption once there. Cliff dismissed the fellow as a waster having nothing helpful to say, and justified his existence on the basis that every organisation seems to have at least one Guy. Charlotte called by, dropping off the key to the cottage for Cliff and said she'd catch-up with them first thing in the morning.

The cottage was a fifteen minute stroll towards the South Light. Built on the outside of Marisco Castle's keep wall, this granite stone building appeared positively substantial compared to his last digs. Aside from a slightly dank feel, Cliff was content that this would be his accommodation for the foreseeable future. A sofa, table and chairs, along with a small well stocked bookcase greeted him, and what he discovered to be a firm double bed completed the picture. It was suitably equipped with a compact kitchenette and small woodburning stove which, by the feel of things, had just been lit. He shifted the pile of white dust sheets from the sofa to one side and made himself comfortable. So much so, within a few minutes he'd fallen asleep. As easily as he had drifted off, he came to his senses, and soon realised he needed the loo. Where on earth was the loo? Urgency overcame Cliff as he scurried about the place hunting for the loo. He found the shower in the bedroom but the loo still evaded him. As a last resort he tried what he took to be an outside porch cupboard. Eureka!

Cliff concluded that the one thing that comes as a surprise can often be the very thing you're looking for. At the end of the day this crime, if indeed there is a crime, is probably only down to just one person, and all he's got to do is find them.

EIGHT

Cliff woke after a sound night to a bright sunny morning. The gloom of the evening before had masked the incredible scene from the cottage, with its large panoramic window overlooking the South Light, the Landing Beach and a distant glimpse of Rat Island, while the side windows in the lounge commanded the most amazing views of the ocean towards the distant mainland.

Busying himself, he rearranged the furniture, propping up a board that had been left on top of the table. On this he could start to piece together the full picture. Up to now it had been like having a blank colouring book but without any crayons. Crucially, experience had shown him that sometimes a suspicion is all you need to help solve a case. In spite of at times forgetting it, he knew full well that he was still a bloody good cop.

'How's it going?' Charlotte greeted the two of them as they entered her office

'What would you say Beer?' Cliff was keen to see how the lad would sum it up.

'Um, quite a mixed bunch. It seemed way over Roy's head until we got to the bones; as for Marion, she turned out to be a rock hugger. Nigel was a real find, especially as he may have met our man up by the Old Lighthouse. Dear Shirley eventually gave us a steer, but Polly's far from happy it would seem with her lot, attractive woman though. Then there was Francesca; they say artists are all over the place but she was something else, and so aggressive. As was Jago, but the boss soon won him over, nice lad. Oh, and the young couple, Tom and er…. Sue, the first real clue in our hands thanks to them. How did I do Boss?' he turned to Cliff hopeful.

'Pretty good son, although you missed out Katrina, Phil and Guy, but otherwise …' Beer beamed.

'Well, it sounds as though it was worthwhile. Between you and me, Polly's on her way and as for Francesca, she's an odd one. She runs art classes in the season for our visitors and they all talk highly of her but I've never taken to her myself. Dear Nigel, he's one of our stalwarts, doesn't miss much and totally reliable.'

'Today I've lined up six more, starting in….' she checked her watch, 'twenty minutes, time enough for a coffee. And Cliff, the Reverend Cleave wants a word, he's living over in Abbotsham but will phone around fiveish. Kenneth's a gem, you'll find him a real help as the priest in charge of Lundy and he's over here every third week in the month, weather permitting.'

'It's interesting Charlotte, how the islanders carry on as if nothing had happened. Do they have a problem trying to relate to something that is not of their world here on Lundy?' Cliff said.

'Trust is a big thing here on the island, it's something that anyone who comes here has to learn. For many it isn't something that comes naturally but we have to be able to trust each other, at times with our life, and protect the very thing that binds us together, the island. You're strangers Cliff, you must understand that and, are in part, a threat to their, our future.'

'Your world is foreign to me, that's why I'm asking.'

Charlotte seized on him, 'Do you not like it?'

'No, it's not that, it's just so different to what I'm used to.'

Beer grabbed the moment, 'Has the island changed much over the years?'

'It has,' Charlotte admitted, 'but maybe not that you would notice.'

Cliff came in sensing the atmosphere, 'I can vouch for that having previously travelled in nothing more than a fishing tub and row boat; not a passenger ship, jetty or helicopter in sight. I'm afraid one change you will see here in the future Charlotte, is the media's attention. When they get hold of the news, they'll be all over you, looking for a tasty story and there's little we can do about it.'

'We understand that and the Trust is concerned, not only about the death, but concerning the long-term damage that will ensue. On a different note Cliff, how's the cottage, will it be alright? You shouldn't be disturbed there.'

'It's great thanks and the views are fantastic. There was only one problem, the solution which I eventually discovered, the outside loo.' Any tension was instantly relieved with laughter.

Of the six remaining interviews the majority offered little help with their enquiries. Josh, a farm and cargo hand had seen nothing suspicious. Mike and Laura Stevens, a middle-aged married couple, had recently moved from the Isle of Mull. They wanted a change of scenery and both agreed they had certainly got that. Mike was the island engineer, working on the power and water systems, as well as on the Land Rovers and ATVs. Clearly well used to long days. Laura, his wife, was the general assistant for the holiday lets and maintenance teams. Neil Bowden was a visiting electrical engineer, working for an Exeter contractor carrying out the annual servicing of the island's heat and power systems. He worked alongside Roy and that just about summed Neil up too.

Bridget, a sprightly mature lady, occupied herself gardening and cleaning. Her love of all things domestic was commendable and hard for the two boys to understand. She shared with them that, on a regular basis, she cleaned the church, a job she absolutely loved. About ten days back she had been aware that someone was using the church to shelter in, unusual, especially at this time of year. She had found discarded chocolate wrappers in the vestry, along with a water bottle and a half eaten peanut bar hidden away; and chairs and a rug had been moved. Bridget had mentioned it to Reverend Cleave who was equally surprised and could only believe it was a visitor on the island.

Di Silva was the Bird Warden for both the Island Trust and the RSPB. At this time of year, she'd hardly see a soul while busy surveying the colonies. A week ago, on her way back from the North End, she came across a man wearing a hoodie, maybe in his thirties, or could have been older, near the Halfway Wall heading south like her. Di asked him if he was okay to which he replied that he was. She thought he had mistaken her to be a visiting bird watcher what with her gear, and said that, being an islander, he was fine and knew his way around. She suggested that, as a fellow nature lover, they could walk together but he declined saying he was going a different way. What made her mention it was that he was no islander.

The Reverend's call to Cliff came through on the dot of five. Respectful of Cliff's position he shared how worried he was. This most recent event had clearly overtaken him and an element of disbelief was plainly evident in his words.

'Are you a praying man officer?'

'I'm God fearing,' Cliff said, 'but I wouldn't say I was much of a prayer as such.'

'Hmm,' the vicar remarked. 'Most come to our island for the wildlife and nature, you're the exception. I guess you've come because of a different kind of nature, man's.'

Cliff couldn't help but feel the minister had a warning to share.

'Evil will come, it is never far from us. What took place in Lundy's past makes the most heinous events of any of England's parishes look like a vicarage tea party.'

Kenneth knew that many islanders had a knowledge of Christian principles but for some, this understanding was mixed with history and superstition, both of which for them, were the very life blood of Lundy.

The vicar's parting words sent a shivering through Cliff.

'In seeking to find the truth amongst the lies, be careful what you search for and, importantly, how you go about it. I am certain we will speak again Detective Cliff and I will pray for you.'

Tucked beside the office phone was an envelope marked to 'Detective Cranford Cliff – Confidential.'

A succinct phone message inside read, 'Ring the doc at 6pm today. Charlie.'

NINE

The doctor slid back one of the substantial steel storage trays loaded with a cadaver and, having slammed its metal door shut, ambled into the autopsy suite. Still wearing his white gown and surgical wellingtons, now decorated with a smattering of grizzly blood spots, he loitered by the telephone. As he waited for it to ring, he tapped on several glass specimen jars in turn, like a child making a choice in a sweet shop. He rubbed his aching eyes, trying to relieve the soreness brought about by concentrating two long under stark white mortuary lamps.

The phone burst into life, 'Doctor Lawrence Cox here. Is that Detective Cranford Cliff?'

'Yep,' stressed Cliff expectantly.

'I have the preliminary findings following the post-mortem and thought you would welcome a heads-up before receiving my full report.'

'Thanks Doc, that's certainly appreciated. I've a pen and note pad so go ahead.'

'Good. As I believe I explained; a fine white foam substance appearing at the nostrils and mouth may well suggest drowning. Minimal amounts were detected and I have sent samples away to the lab for analysis. A typical indicator of drowning is ingestion of water into the air passages and subsequently lungs and blood as the victim struggles, choking. There is no evidence of a pre-death struggle in the water with no signs of anoxia present. The post-mortem did not reveal the lungs as being pale and distended, nor were they heavy. No water was present in any quantity in the stomach and oesophagus and no sea debris was evident, nor the presence of anything but a few diatoms, natural microscopic organisms. It is true that sudden and unexpected plunging into cold water can cause 'reflex cardiac arrest,' in which case the signs of drowning will not be present. Not common however, in someone in their forties, fifties. I must advise you that examination of his heart led me to believe no such cardiac inhibition transpired and I can confirm he did not die from natural causes.

'The majority of drownings of adults occur in connection with shipping and boating accidents, or drunk or drugged individuals falling into water. Following initial screening our John Doe had no alcohol or drugs in his bloodstream, or needle marks, nor did I discover any evidence of an infectious disease. Obviously, the presence of injuries to the body and head, of which they are extensive, might be caused either exclusively, or in part, by the many hazards the body may have encountered; rocks, submerged obstacles, collision with a craft, even animals and not excluding a fall from the land or a boat. The appearance of wounds can be misleading because changes in the blood caused by water makes it difficult to ascertain with confidence whether injuries were received before or after death. In my opinion, however, the head injuries to the skull, particularly to the back of the head, were caused by a blow from a blunt instrument.'

The doc cleared his throat, 'So, in summary, I could not confidently rule out that foul play was not involved in his death. Off the record Cliff, I'm more certain that if you chaps rule out a suicide leap by an already dead man,' he chuckled, 'you're looking at a murder!'

Cliff's brain went into overdrive, 'Right.'

'I'm forwarding my initial path report, plus photographs and documentary material, direct to the Coroner's Office and I'll copy you guys in.'

'I want to get the police artist on this case in an attempt for a facial recognition, if she needs more photographs can she contact you, Doc?'

'Sure thing. I'd say he appears to be between 40 and 45 years if that's helpful? When a person dies their body cells and hair, for example, remain active for a time, that may prove useful for identification. The coroner will now take custody of the body as with any unexplained death, as we attempt to discover who the victim is and what actually happened. If necessary, he can call on an additional pathologist who specialises in drowning incidents, but we'll wait on that one. Should the victim be identified, then the coroner will have the responsibility to trace and contact any relatives, but I'm sure you know that Cliff. I doubt that time will be on our side for any organ or tissue donations. Obviously, I will contact you should I learn anything more and rest assured, the few bits collected on the beach at the scene, along with test samples and body parts have all been securely stored and preserved.

'One finding I wanted to enlighten you on which might be of interest Cliff, is that his left wrist showed a paling impression of what looked like a watch, where one had been worn. It suggested to me, not conclusively I must add, that he'd been stripped. My experience is that most who undress to commit suicide wouldn't take their watch off. It's far too personal a belonging to discard, it's second nature to leave it on, not for someone else to have. I don't want to muddy the waters so to speak but you've got to appreciate my job is all about being suspicious.

'To my knowledge there has never before been a murder enquiry on Lundy, that is apart from a floater, some Italian single-handed sailor who was washed up on the Landing Beach. Subsequently, it was concluded he had fallen unconscious overboard from his nearby yacht. Best of luck with this one Cliff.'

Dr Laurence Cox, MB, BMSc, FRCPath, MFFLM appeared much like any other addicted academic as he puffed a pipe of Golden Virginia, adorned with his full surgical garb, complete with grizzly congealed, blood stains. The pipe aroma helped mask the clinging odour of raw meat on him. He had persisted with Woodbine cigarettes but they would die out on him if he didn't keep puffing. As he sucked his pipe, he concluded that Woodbines, or a pipe for that matter, would probably be the death of him, but there were far worse ways to go.

TEN

A neat looking young chap sat at a desk, his navy trousers pressed with knife like creases, a sparkling white ironed shirt peeked from beneath a beige cardigan which was topped with a creased corduroy jacket. In addition, a pair of gleaming black shoes and a knitted mustard coloured tie completed his outfit which served as a testament to a past era. Andrew Maunder had been in post as a junior reporter at The Journal for fourteen months. Wisely in moments of crisis he would look for guidance to his older, more experienced colleague but unfortunately on this day, Stan was away from the office treating his ailing mother to a fortnight in Eastbourne, likely her final swan song. Conrad, the editor, was equally indisposed at The Royal North Devon Golf Club, the oldest course in England, now challenging one of its oldest over par members.

So, it was when the anonymous call came into the paper that day, declaring a dead body had been discovered on Lundy, that Andrew took the call. He couldn't believe what he was hearing as the caller breathlessly spared no gruesome detail, and quickly Andrew appreciated this was his best chance to make a name with the biggest 'hard news story' ever. Even anonymous calls to the paper prompted a degree of research to ascertain their validity, ensuring they weren't dealing with a con or a malicious lie. For him to get this past Conrad he needed to fill in the background and pretty damn quick. After due consideration over no more than ten or so minutes, just long enough to brew a cuppa, Andrew took the bull by the horns and phoned Bideford Nick. Following what seemed an inordinate delay holding on for their switchboard to answer, the woman finally put him through.

'Sergeant Charlie Harris, who am I speaking to and how can I help?'

Following introductions Andrew opted for a direct approach.

Charlie listened then said, 'Well, I don't know where you got that idea . .' he paused waiting for an answer. 'Oh, I see. Well, you chaps are the first to know folk come up with all manner of weird and wonderful ideas to get in the paper. Can you put Conrad on?'

Andrew mumbled something about a meeting.

'I see, well Stan then.'

There was a brief delay before Andrew admitted he was the only one on the news team in the office.

'It's good you were in… it's Maunder, is it? Get Conrad to call me on his return and I'll clear up any misunderstanding.'

While repeatedly tapping his biro on the desktop Andrew reconsidered their brief conversation and realised that the officer hadn't specifically denied the claim.

Easing back in his office chair he rubbed his neck wishing his mother didn't insist on using starch on his collars. He knew if this story was going to fly, he needed hard facts that would stand Conrad's scrutiny, and he needed them now.

'Someone's contacted the press, they're on it; the media circus is on its way Cliff. Good luck.'

Charlie's telephone call didn't come as a surprise but it made Cliff's heart sink as he knew that in no time, they'd be all over it; just what wasn't needed.

In a funny kind of way Cliff respected Charlie. Sure, Charlie could be at times a trifle pedantic in upholding the dated methods of policing but nevertheless he was sharp enough to spot the subtlest of detail that others might overlook. Irrespective of how long it took, Charlie rarely missed the opportunity to catch his man and get them up before the local beak. Unfortunately, his reliance on diktats in preference to staff engagement and encouragement did little to improve Charlie's man-management skills.

On the occasions when Cliff found Charlie particularly irritating, it would have been so easy to remind the old boy that he'd very nearly lost his job in the Force. Charlie, when pressed, described the incident as being something and nothing, a stupid fling with a rookie WPC after an office bash. Cliff appreciated he was the last person to judge a fellow officer, a superior at that, in spite of, at times, wanting to.

Cliff's experience of extra marital affairs was very much second hand. He thought his marriage to Suzanna,

69

seven years his junior, was working well. Each week he got out with the lads down the local for a pint or two and a round of darts. He helped organise the Youth Boxing Club and there would be the occasional weekend following Arsenal's away matches. Throughout it all Suzanna was always undemanding, punctual with his meals and meticulous about the home. He had noticed over time her social programme had become busier, fuller, more unpredictable. With regard to the physical aspects of their marriage he couldn't but be aware of her increased levels of tiredness. Suzanna, meanwhile, considered that their relationship was dead in the water. So, it was more than coincidental that through the local tennis club she met a wealthy bachelor farmer from Hertfordshire and eventually took off with him and his 263 Holstein Friesians. In truth, the big difference between Charlie and Cliff was Charlie's Mabel had him back, while Cliff never saw Suzanna again except for their court settlement hearing. For Cliff, the whole episode was one he didn't like to talk about or be reminded of.

P.C. Beer was puzzled by Cliff's move to the sticks away from the buzz and thrills of London.

'What made you move to Devon Boss?

Cliff had been embarrassed to admit to friends and colleagues that his wife had walked out on him, it did little to bolster his image. The fact that it was in preference to a cow farmer over and above a crime fighter was the last straw. In one sense it was fortuitous there were no children, but there again, Suzanna's departure meant he was alone, trying somehow to manage a massive mortgage, way beyond the bounds of his constable's wage. His new undesirable circumstances left few options. Westcountry real estate was financially a very different story to that of London, so a new start was initiated with the purchase of a small cottage located in the back alleys of the small coastal village of Appledore, and as fortune would have it, a stone's throw from The Beaver.

The move necessitated a new minimalistic approach greatly challenging his natural instinct for collecting. He'd never seen this as a problem until now. For him it was adopting a responsible attitude to a sustainable lifestyle, one which ensured that no matter what Cliff might want, he had it somewhere. He never considered that this practice had a part to play in their marriage break-up, reassuring himself that Suzanna simply didn't like living in London and loved animals. Well, something along those lines. In truth she had long since become disillusioned with her marriage, finding Cliff increasingly boring. His new start in North Devon created the opportunity to avoid sharing details of his past domestic arrangements with anyone. Quickly colleagues learnt to stop asking but alas no one had been charitable enough to brief P.C. Beer.

'Are you married Sir?'

Unsurprisingly Cliff greatly missed the luxury of having a woman about the house, tending to his significant and well established needs. Returning at the end of the day to an empty, untidy house and no meal on the table came hard to him; although he did wonder how he could cope considering someone else after all these years.

'I was Constable, but I'd rather leave it at that.'

Although inexperienced Beer knew well enough when to change the subject, certain Cliff was choosing to keep something from him.

ELEVEN

Beer was without doubt a son of Devon, born and bred. Having rarely left the county, he knew little of the world, that is apart from family holidays in adjoining Somerset's Butlins at Minehead. The village of Shirwell near Barnstaple was his family's home. If it was good enough for the adventurer Sir Francis Chichester, it was bound to be good enough for him, not that he knew who Sir Francis was. This lanky, curly fair-haired youth, sporting a pale as death complexion, boasted a persona that was easy to ignore. His unaccomplished educational upbringing had little to commend itself to a boy who allegedly hardly applied himself. Every minute of Beer's free time was spent on a local small holding practising being a farmer. In the mind of this moderately shy and nervously disposed young man, he'd be more than happy if this was to be his destiny. Unsurprisingly, a career in the Devon and Cornwall Constabulary had never occurred to this thoroughly decent old fashioned youth, but as many can bear witness, unpredictable developments can bring about dramatic changes in one's life and future.

'I've spoken with CID, and Jack said he's checked regional Missing Persons, and there's no case vaguely matching our John Doe. If we get the artist's picture over to him, he may have more luck, but wasn't holding out much hope. The Coastguard are coming back to Doreen regarding tidal conditions, but at present can't identify any unusual shipping movements off Lundy over the period of a month prior, and they had no reported incidents.'

Beer looked up from his note-book. 'Have you any good news boss?'

Cliff had been silent long enough.

'We certainly need some that's for sure.'

'Oh, the watch!' Beer recalled proudly, 'the one with the broken strap that the young couple found on the cliff top.'

Cliff nodded, 'I'm not sure what they were doing to discover a watch in the paradise of damp tussocks of grass; maybe observing the birds, seals or, more probably, the barnacles and limpets. No matter, it's one of our few clues, go on.'

'Well, it proved not to be a cheap watch but a rather swanky Omega.'

'So?' Cliff's word showed an air of impatience and lack of knowledge of Omegas.

'We got our friendly jeweller in Barnstaple to have a look. Thankfully it is a genuine model which means it will be etched with a unique serial number on the case or movement, this serves as a fingerprint, providing a way to identify the specific watch, its model, year of production and maybe a possibility to trace when and where it was sold. He has a contact who is helping to ascertain its exact history.' Beer closed his notebook with a sense of satisfaction.

'Well done. It's a priority Beer. We need to conclusively link it to our body. Let's hope the doc will be able to help on that front and pray our guy was the one who originally bought it. Stay on top of that one, well done.'

Beer felt well chuffed.

'Charlotte tells me some biddy wants to see me, a...' Cliff referred to a piece of paper, 'a Professor Beryl Flambard, she led the island search party. Oh, and Sarge wants transcripts of the interviews, you better get your memory as well as your pen working, there's always procedures Beer. I'll keep notes on the Prof and remaining interviews; never let it be said I dumped you in it!' and he all but laughed.

Judging the Professor's age was hard; Cliff assessed that she was in her seventies, if not early eighties. Beryl's rounded face was furnished with a head of tightly cropped, dark brown hair, coloured Cliff concluded. A chubby chin perched below her bulbous nose blended almost seamlessly into her wrinkled neck, whilst her distinctive rounded form was dressed in a black turtleneck sweater beneath a thick blue cardigan, brown worsted trousers and almost matching tweed jacket. The ensemble was completed with a narrow gold chain necklace and brightly coloured trainers. In Cliff's eyes she couldn't look more the part.

Beryl spoke slowly, deliberately and fastidiously, accompanying her words with frequent head movements from side to side seemingly stretching her neck. Her whole demeanour appeared somewhat pained.

'I needed an urgent word. It's not something I would wish to share with others. It's regarding our coastal search. Over the years I've spent much time heading up the work of the society, The Lundy Field Society. Our aims are the study and conservation of the island. So, I know Lundy and its inhabitants well - very few know them better.'

Cliff was wondering when she was going to get to the point. Beryl suspected as much.

'Three of us walked the island; Rosemary, Douglas and of course, myself. Just as you didn't know what if anything we might discover, nor did we. Yet we found nothing out of the ordinary, that's the truth I am afraid, but…'

'Go on,' Cliff warmly encouraged.

'I wouldn't usually talk about someone behind their back but when we were out, Rosemary pressed me to tell her if anything was found. You see, there were times when we split up and went off searching by ourselves. I thought it was an odd request so asked her why, why did she need to know? She was reluctant to say but I wasn't giving her the option. It happens that she didn't but someone else did and asked her to find out.'

'Did she tell you who?'

'No!'

'Any idea why anyone would want to know that, Beryl?'

'None at all. Rosemary's a lovely woman but don't get me wrong, she's quite a timid soul and keen to please.'
Beryl fidgeted, moving her head from side to side once again and now appeared nervous.

'Did you want to say something else?'

She sat bolt upright, as if a rod had been rammed suddenly down her back and spoke in a shaky voice, 'This incident has changed things. Lundy is no longer what it was. Folks love and trust their life here but all that's at risk. I want us to be as we were! I am aware of the crisis we all face, yet fear there are those for whom this will prove too much; the loss of trust, and the island no longer a place of tranquillity and peace.'

She moved uneasily, 'You have a responsibility to find who did this because if you don't, they may not stop, that's the worry, and the life we've grown to love here on Lundy, everything about it, is at risk.'

A long silence hung in the room. She didn't need to say anything more but carried on, 'Here you can look up to the sky at night and see only millions of stars, God's magnificence; nothing of the world's over indulgence polluting this place. That's the world that we cherish and don't want to lose, mustn't lose.'

Cliff couldn't help but notice, even in just the few clear evenings he'd been on the island, the spectacular night skies and the brilliance of the stars; but also, the mass of distant piercing lights on the mainland.

'How did the chat go Boss, did you learn anything new?'

'Truly nothing I didn't already suspect, that is except we have someone else who's keen to know about our investigations.'

'Who?'

'That's for us to discover Beer, along with the reason why. By the way, I've just had faxed through the artist's composite picture illustrating JD's facial features based on the mortuary photographs, a likeness which we can use to show islanders and the public during our enquiries. What do you think?' he asked handing it to Beer.

'Pretty darn good! Anyone would think they were a professional artist.'

'They are, you idiot.' Cliff shared jovially, 'they work with publishers and magazines. I've got the doc to forward the drawing and photographs to Jack in CID. He tells me he's sending through our deceased's Oral Structures Report which will help us confirm identification if we have access to a suspect's ante-mortem dental chart. He's tried to be as thorough as possible to give us the best chance and included a Dental Practitioner's Dental Record and diagrammatic charts, radiographs and his examinations commentary. Doc's made moulds of the teeth should future comparisons or referrals to specialists be necessary. He says, if needs be we could adopt genetic fingerprinting, it would prove more reliable than the old ink and roller method, what with the state of the deceased's fingers. Certainly, he believes studying the blood is the best foolproof option for a positive identification.'

Beer recalled he'd seen something about it on a BBC's Tomorrow's World programme.

'Aren't we talking weeks to process the results Boss?'

'Doc assures me that with the new digital DNA profiling it can be as fast as a couple of days.'

Just then another thought came to Cliff, 'What was the outcome regarding the missing passenger?'

Beer considered briefly, 'Oh yes,' he flicked through his note book, 'I contacted the Island Office at Bideford Quay who got Frank to call me back. The passenger definitely didn't return to Bideford on his return ticket, or for that matter on the Ilfracombe Harbour route. There were twenty passengers on the sailing, so Frank's going to check with the ship's crew who were on that day in case anyone can recall him. The Quay Booking Office are trying to retrieve any payment records but were instantly able to trace the name that the booking was made in.'

Beer hesitated, 'John Smith.'

Cliff reluctantly asserted, 'That could indeed be our man, but not his name.'

TWELVE

Douglas McIntyre was a friendly, small chatty fellow, rarely seen without his flat cap. He had been retired from a colourful career working in local garages. His wife had died about eight years back, shortly after which, Douglas considered it was time for a dramatic change in his life. One of eight children, three of his siblings survive and now live within a few miles of their family home in Northam. Douglas missed strolling the sun-kissed beaches of Westward Ho! and Instow people watching, and fondly recalled his youth, travelling far and wide on the North Devon lanes searching out dances and local talent. But now this elderly gent had made Lundy his home.

The remoteness that Lundy offered was hardly anything new for Douglas who'd spent much of his childhood being dragged here and there by his father to experience the joys of wilderness camping. His father found it hard not to share his wartime exploits of serving on the Norwegian Northern Front with his son. Douglas could imagine that the self-same sun that rested over the distant Atlantic horizon beyond Lundy, as having also cast its pink light over the snow covered mountains and blue green waters of Northern Norway's Fjords all those years before. Island life for Douglas followed a strict pattern, with little change. He never shunned hard work, nor cut corners in whatever he did: repairing tractors, cars, machinery; undertaking odd jobs on the estate's buildings and maintenance of the drystone walling, which was extensive. His main relaxation was following premier football. In his early island days, he and a handful of lads would have a boot around up on the tent field, but that was beyond him now.

Cliff was first to speak, 'Thanks Douglas for helping us with the search of the island, something that both Beer here and I are hardly fit for.'

Beer didn't let that go easily, 'Boss!'

'Well, I'm not anyway,' Cliff obliged. 'We'd be interested to hear what brought you to Lundy and as to whether you've spotted anything unusual recently, on your travels so to speak?'

Douglas needed no further encouragement, 'You see, living on the mainland I increasingly felt stressed, out of place; but here, here on Lundy, my life has changed. I feel in balance with nature and the breath-taking heart of this unspoilt ancient island. You'd be forgiven for thinking this is a barren land, but far from it. Each spring it bursts into life and colour; I love it.'

'You're a part of the Field Group?' Beer said.

'Yes. Much of the island is a triple SI and our waters, Britain's first Marine Nature Reserve.'

'And there's the puffins?' Beer persisted.

'Sure, but I'm more of a big mammal man myself.' He could see the officers looked a bit unsure. 'Deer and ponies. The Japanese Sika deer thrive here. I love to catch them hiding on the east side, or grazing and running free over the open farmland in the early dawn or at dusk, their brown coats and dappled white spots magically catching the sunlight. We've fifty or so Lundy ponies grazing on the island. A rare breed, a cross between the Welsh Mountain and New Forest stock. It's a wonderful sight to see them as a herd running together. I'm not turned on by the goats but they do help to keep the gorse and shrubbery down. From March on, we see our summer migrant birds take up home here and thousands upon thousands pass through the island in the autumn. It's a twitcher's paradise. Beryl, and the rest of us organise guided walks during the year on most boat days throughout the season, and she gives talks in the Tavern.'

Douglas paused, the boys unsure if for breath or in thought, 'I can remember as a lad,' he resumed, 'when the White Funnel steamers used to run, we'd often see dolphins and porpoises follow the ships. Now I can catch a glimpse of a basking shark or two and the occasional whale… This is now my world,' he shared with more than a hint of emotion.

The boys had let him ramble, not because it was vital information, just that they'd been captivated by his story.

'I'm sorry, you've let me rabbit on, I know I can be boring at times.'

Cliff immediately put him right, 'Not at all, we've been enthralled Douglas - isn't that right Beer?'

'Beer said, 'Yep, that's right.'

'You asked detective, if I'd noticed anything unusual. Well over the past weeks, I've been shifting some hefty rocks rebuilding the corner anchor stones on the cemetery walls. Some, I have had to roll in place as they are too heavy to lift. The cottage is but a stone's throw away, so to speak, from where I was working. Close enough to hear raised voices, although not what was said. It seemed unusual because it occurred several times when I was up there working, over perhaps four or five days.'

'So, what made you mention it?' Cliff persisted.

'There's only one person in the cottage and she lives on her own.'

Beer ventured, 'Maybe she had someone staying with her, someone she didn't get on with?'

'No way,' Douglas replied emphatically. 'Whilst arguing wouldn't be out of character, she'd never have anyone to stay with her.'

'What's the cottage?' Cliff mused.

'Stoneycroft. It's where the lighthouse inspectors use to stay when they visited the island; it stands alongside the Old Light.'

'Could you have confused it with voices from the Old Light?' Cliff continued.

'Absolutely not; it's too far away, and anyway, empty. No, it was definitely from the cottage, a man and a woman's voice.'

'And someone lives there?' Beer confirmed.

The pitch of Douglas' voice rose as he affirmed, 'Yes, and it's her art studio.'

Rosemary Smart proved a totally different kettle of fish. Lacking confidence, nervous, shy, fearful and shrinking; this seemed to sum Rosemary to a tee for Cliff, and Beryl's description of her as being a 'timid soul,' was spot on. Cliff presumed to let Beer take the lead, not too challenging for her he considered.

'Firstly, thanks Rosemary for going to the trouble of helping to search the island the other day, it's much appreciated.'

She was clearly taken aback and responsive to the gesture. 'Oh, it was nothing really, I enjoy spending time close to the island's nature.'

'Sure,' Beer agreed, 'and what particularly is your forte…your interest?'

Without a moment's thought she said, 'The puffins. I love the puffins.'

You've got her thought Cliff.

'Right, I can understand that,' Beer agreed, 'the island I guess wouldn't be the same without the sight and sound of hundreds of puffins wheeling and sweeping about the cliffs. They're so charming, aren't they?'

'There aren't the hundreds we once had, but the numbers are growing slowly. It's enchanting to observe the antics of their courtship, bill tapping and to see the young, ungainly chicks emerge from their burrow weeks later. They're so endearing. I spend hours watching them grow until they eventually take to the air and join the adult flocks out at sea.'

She appeared to be in a moment of reflection.

'That sounds amazing,' Cliff said.

'Of course, you'll have to come back next spring if you want to see them.'

'Right,' Beer said. 'We had hoped that if something had been discovered, or cropped-up, we could have finalised our investigations and left you all in peace.'

'Nothing did turn up, did it?' There was a hint of the need for reassurance in how she spoke.

'I'm sure that's a relief to some?' said Beer.

'Yes, I suppose.'

'Anybody in particular?'

She thought, 'I guess so.'

'Out of interest did anyone show a particular interest in the search Rosemary?'

The boys weren't certain that she hadn't been expecting this.

'Well, one seemed intent to know when it would be over,' she stopped there.

'I can understand that,' Beer concurred, 'in a similar situation I'd probably feel the same. Who was that?'

They left her to make the next move. Moments passed.

'I don't really know why, but Shirley was keen to know.'

'And when you told her it had been fruitless, how did she react?' Cliff waited.

'That's the strange thing,' Rosemary explained, 'she seemed pleased.'

THIRTEEN

The day started bright and dry.

'A coffee,' Cliff declared, 'and we can catch up.'

'It's not all that private where I am.' Beer said.

'No. I had in mind the Tavern. You could ensure Shirley's undisturbed by others while I chat to her'

The bar was eerily empty. There was distant faint music from a transistor and he could hear lively talk coming from the kitchen. The chatter turned out to be more words of annoyance. As the boys entered the kitchen's tension confronted them. An exasperated Shirley was letting rip at Polly who appeared to be cowering in a corner, slumped over, head in hands.

'Sorry ladies, hope we're not interrupting but wanted a word if that's okay Shirley; in private?' Cliff said while noticing Polly's disturbed demeanour. 'I'll tell you what,' and with that he looked to Beer, 'if you have a bit of a chat with Polly in the bar about what we discussed, I'll grab a coffee with Shirley here. What do you say?' he directed to Shirley but didn't wait for a response. 'Good, that's settled,' and in no time the predicament was defused.

Beer looked uncertain but nevertheless, seized the opportunity, for this was the spirited young woman he'd encountered before, although her spirit today seemed sadly lacking. Polly didn't look up but just knowingly followed Beer out, like some captive who had been spared their own execution.

Seated opposite each other in the bar Beer spoke. The girl seemed preoccupied, disinterested, unwilling to talk. She murmured something which Beer couldn't make out.

He tried again, louder. 'Does no one talk normally here?' Beer said. 'Can I pour you a cocktail or a whisky?'

She looked at him, her usually pretty face painfully contorted. Then he noticed thin white wires trailing from each ear connected to buds, which were busily filling her head with noise.

'Sorry. The old bag goes on endlessly, she's better once she's had a rant,' Polly confessed as she pulled the buds out and tucked them and their leads in the top of her partly unbuttoned shirt. Beer had raised his hand to his mouth, a unconscious act, which he did when at a loss.

'I'm all yours…officer!' she said shaking herself out of her melancholia.

It was then he realised, as he cradled his chin in his hand, that he hadn't shaved for a while. Briefly he considered that perhaps he should grow a beard, then instantly dismissed the ridiculous idea.

'So, Shirley,' Cliff said.
She looked uneasy.

'A couple of coffees, eh? I wanted to ask you about the island search.'

Shirley filled the kettle and plugged it in. Cliff thought she was about to say something, but he decided to hold the conversation.

'I know you didn't go on the island search, but I gather you were keen to know how it went, and particularly if anything was found. I'm interested to know why?'

'That's my business.' She responded so quickly it was as if she had anticipated the question.

Cliff was having none of it, 'And Shirley, that's my business now!'

Shirley could tell he wasn't going to let it go.

'I can't say.' And with that, fumbled with the jar scooping a spoon of coffee into each mug.

'White? Sugar?' she said in a monotone voice.

'Just white,' Cliff accommodated her.

She moved uneasily, and offered only a shrug, clearly determined not to say.

Charlotte stood alone on the cliff top just below Castle Keep Cottage, gazing towards the South Light and out to sea. She loved wonderful days like this when her island rested peaceful and still in the noon day sun. From her vantage point she could, on occasions, observe the Oldenburg making headway on high water towards the island. With the sun glistening on the azure sea, one could be forgiven for thinking everything was normal. However, as she struggled to remain optimistic a sense of foreboding overcame her and she began to consider the events of the past few days.

'Hi yer!' cried out to her.

She turned round and recognised Cliff standing by the cottage doorway. A warm breeze kissed her face.

'You okay Charlotte? Do you want a coffee?'

She knew it would be impossible to share how she felt, he'd never understand.

He beckoned to her, 'I'll pop the kettle on.'

Ever since Cliff arrived on the island, she had watched him battling his prejudices, trying to come to terms with his own past and future, as well as that of Lundy.

Curious, he asked whilst gathering the mugs and milk, 'What's wrong, Charlotte?'

'Oh nothing,' she said; and knowing it would hardly reassure him, deftly changed the subject, 'How are the investigations going?'

'We're progressing...' he considered 'it's slower than I'd wish but I'm not surprised.'

She gave him a quizzical look.

'My experience tells me that in any case there's always something more than meets the eye, and that's what I'm banking on,' he said.

Cliff could see she was at a loss.

'You see, I'm looking for a murderer - it was no accident. Someone had reason to do him in, any ideas? And, by the way, who's the person who tipped-off the papers? They are squarely in my cross hairs.'

'Maybe it's getting on top of you, the island I mean ... island life, us?'

'No way,' Cliff came straight back, 'you couldn't have been more understanding and helpful. It would have been a struggle without your support.'

'You know if there's more I can do, I'm here. I know everyone, what they get up to and, importantly, I have their confidence. We're not used to this kind of excitement on Lundy you know?'

Cliff jerked awkwardly, moving back on the sofa nearly spilling his coffee; he spontaneously raised his hand to his chest.

'Are you okay?'

All manner of horrendous thoughts crashed through her mind. Cliff raised his face and managing a meagre smile, nodded. He could see panic in her eyes.

'It's my ticker, it's a bit jumpy, occasionally it misses a cog or two. I suffer with arrhythmia, an abnormal heart rhythm, nothing to worry about,' he tried to reassure her but she wasn't convinced. 'I take blockers.'

Charlotte took his hand from his chest and as she did, his heart began to steady. Their fingers momentarily entwined. Looking her in the eye, he saw her somehow differently.

In an attempt to relieve the tension, he made it clear it didn't stop him doing his job, his duty as he described it.

Anxious for him, she seized the opportunity, 'Duty will always be awaiting you but health and happiness won't.'

Acknowledging reluctantly the change of mood she said, 'Cliff, what on earth ever made you want to be a policeman?' Charlotte was uncertain how truthful an answer she'd get.

'It's funny, but I always had this desire to catch the crook, the villain and murderer. Ever since watching TV crime dramas, that had been my ambition to catch the bast…' he refrained. 'You see they're never as bright as they'd like you to believe they are; well, that's how it was on TV. But no matter how clever they are, they still make mistakes and that's where I come in.'

'So, what gives them away, the murderers?' She had the bit firmly between her teeth.

Cliff smiled. Charlotte waited.

'For most the risks are so high it's hard to keep a lid on it. It could be an error, an oversight, a detail, maybe just a wrong word. I imagine the pressure must be tremendous in keeping it a secret, they'd need to be on top of their game all the time and most aren't.' Cliff considered, 'And of course there's those murders that aren't planned, they've got to be so much the harder to keep secret.'

'And our murderer?' There was a sadness in her voice.

'I'm really not sure,' Cliff said. 'I know about the murderers that have been caught; there are plenty who haven't but that's not my intention for our one.'

Charlotte realised the time for small chat had long passed, Cliff's thoughts were now on pursuing the killer.

What neither of them knew however, was that shortly to disembark from the Oldenburg was, amongst others, one Andrew Maunder, enthusiastically ready to uncover the darkest and grimmest of secrets in his search for a story. The story that would make his name.

FOURTEEN

The ship's crew were only too conscious of the reporter's endeavours to secure his scoop. Throughout much of their sailing he'd been asking all manner of questions, delving into the mystery.

'We don't have the luxury of The Journal being overendowed with staff, especially with Stan, our senior reporter, away,' Conrad had explained to Andrew before he had left.

'As well as writing up those stories handed on to you, sometimes you need to get out there and find your own. I certainly have no appetite to go chasing across the ocean, building bridges with locals on some godforsaken island on the off chance of a scoop.'

Conrad, determined to leave Andrew in no doubt, spelt it out for him. 'Being a reporter is rather like being a hound sniffing around not knowing exactly what you're going to find until you've discovered it. Once discovered all you have to do is make sense of it and see how it fits into the bigger picture. Remember it's an honourable trade. How you interpret the facts is uniquely down to you Andrew, you have the obligation to share all you discover. Stick to the truth, follow the facts, paint the picture and let the story tell itself. Be cautious, gossip spreads like wild-fire up here in North Devon and even faster I suspect on a tiny island like Lundy where there ain't a lot of news.'

Andrew recalled Conrad's final words, 'You must stay focussed on the detail; striving to collect, verify and analyse the facts, and only then tell the story, if indeed one exists, which I doubt. It will be an ideal opportunity to test your persistence and determination. No better training.'

I'm not just a reporter, he thought to himself as he stood on the deck of the ship. I'm an investigator, a revealer - he liked the sound of that. He looked about himself; a youth was tapping frantically at his mobile, attempting Andrew assumed, to get a signal on his black Nokia which seemed to be getting nothing more than a spasmodic signal. A lass standing by the youth looked suitably bored, staring hopelessly out to sea. The recollection of a past relationship flashed through Andrew's mind, which he discounted as swiftly as it arrived. A giggly couple of young love-birds twittered about their expectations of the island as they paraded about the deck, oblivious of everyone it seemed.

'It's turned out to be a fine day and crossing,' a thirty-something woman presumed to share with Andrew, 'flat calm, ideal. I thought we'd be more crowded than this.'
At first glance this self-confessed bird watcher came across as frumpy, old fashioned and a tad simple or naïve.

They chatted awhile, comparing notes on each of their forthcoming stay-overs on Lundy. She was particularly taken with Andrew's exciting challenge.

Andrew had not banked on such a demanding climb up to the village. No matter how much research one does some facts will always evade one, he thought. As they talked, he began to wonder just how much his new companion knew about birds. His knowledge on the hobby was scant to say the least, but she seemed positively evasive and vague on the subject saying she knew now was the best time of year to glimpse the puffins! Strange, he thought.

FIFTEEN

While Andrew's fellow intrepid travellers set off from the village in all directions to explore the island, he decided to settle in The Marisco Tavern, convinced that here he'd catch the latest gossip.

'Are you a reporter? The North Devon Journal?'
A flustered young Andrew Maunder acknowledged the presumption.

Gingerly he enquired, 'And you are?'

'Detective Cranford Cliff, Devon and Cornwall Constabulary,' Cliff shared with a degree of authority and sufficiently loudly to be clearly heard over the noise of lunch time diners.

'I'll be frank,' Cliff said offering a false smile, 'I wouldn't say your arrival is anything of a surprise or that you're unwelcome for that matter, but that's assuming you don't create waves and frustrate my investigations. I don't think you said who you are?' he smiled again.

'Oh, Andrew Maunder,' the lad shared with a degree of nervousness.

'What exactly are you hoping to do while you're here Andrew? How long are you staying?'

'A couple of days,' he said apologetically.

'Fine. So how are you planning to get off the island?'

'My boss has chartered a fishing boat to pick me up and get me back to Clovelly…that's if the weather's okay.'

'That's Conrad, is it?'

'Yes, that's him,' he said a little taken aback.

'I understand he had a call to Charlie at Bideford Nick and they agreed it's logical to work together, we're neighbours after all and collaboration has worked in the past. I'll speak plainly; it's essential the islanders feel confident to confide in me, the last thing I need is an inexperienced reporter full of innocent endeavours and bravado stirring things up and creating problems. Have I made myself clear?'

'Completely,' Andrew said, 'I would be keen to look to you for guidance.'

'We should get on okay then. It may well be you'll learn things that they wouldn't tell me or my constable, so I'm expecting you to run everything past me.'

'Sure, maybe we can compare notes?'

'Maybe,' Cliff stated, 'and I'll liaise with you over what The Journal can print at this stage in our enquiries. Right!' Andrew was left in no doubt regarding their future working relationship and encouraged they'd got off to such a good start. Meanwhile Cliff knew sooner or later they'd be needing the press to help ID their man.

'How was your sailing, Andrew? Ours was pretty choppy.'

Andrew gave a brief account, outlining in some detail his fellow passengers. Feeling he was already somehow being tested he explained about the woman, the odd reluctant 'so called' bird watcher. Cliff was impressed with the lad's powers of observation and more than interested in the woman, asking Andrew to see what more he could learn about her.

'What was it like when you first saw the body, detective?'

Cliff temporarily cast his mind back. 'It's still a shock when you find a dead body, even if you're expecting it.'

'I've a confession to make,' Andrew admitted. Conscious of Cliff's reaction and searching glare he continued, 'From the moment I had the tip off I hoped it would prove to be a murder. That's dreadful, isn't it?'

'I'm afraid so, but there again that's more of a reflection on the jobs we do than us. You're the first here Andrew, but I can tell you, not for long. Just remember what we agreed and I'll get Constable Beer to give you some background.'

'Jago's fit for the caves,' Beer said, interrupting Cliff's train of thought. 'He's got the Land Rover if we want to go now?'

Cliff's immediate thought was to consider how much more appealing that was than the hike, certainly back-up from the Landing Beach.

'The island's riddled with caves and there's a fair few near the beach,' Jago shared as they bounced down the track.

'There's one I particularly want to show you, see what you think?'

He was sufficiently mysterious, arousing a degree of inquisitiveness in the boys. Getting out of the vehicle he explained that there was a small cave 20 metres up a very steep precipice below the castle, that in the early days was used for smuggled bounty and hiding convicts who should have been shipped to America. Jago had checked it out but it seemed blocked with just rubbish and told them he didn't think their man would have even known it was there. What he really wanted them to see was one of the smaller caves, off the main track, which had been hacked out into the cliff, overlooking the beach. Being high enough to stand upright in, the cave ran some 10 yards back. As they entered, water dripped upon them from the salt laden chamber's roof. Musty dank air hung heavy inside.

'Whose is the boat?' Beer ventured.

'It's here if needed, for any islander to use.'

The fibre glass row dingy was a mere three metres long, propped against the cave's wall with a pair of wooden oars.

'A bit knocked around.' Cliff added.

'Sure, but a reasonable freeboard and plenty stable enough if it's calm,' Jago enlightened.

'So?' a puzzled Cliff remarked.

'When chatting to the crew, two of the lads said they noticed her being rowed south, round Mouse and Rat Islands towards Surf Point. They couldn't make out who the person was rowing but they were making reasonable headway and they assumed out for exercise, maybe to catch sight of seals or a basker. Anyway, it was unusual as the boat's only normally used in the bay, the more sheltered waters. They thought nothing of it until we got chatting about the body.' Jago waited.

Cliff spoke first, 'A man or a woman; could they see?'

Jago frowned, 'They couldn't really be sure but thought, a man.'

Beer said, 'Surf Point, where's that?'

'It's the Island's most easterly point, below the bay. You'd need to round it, rowing through the broken tidal waters of the Race to reach the south coast and the back beach of Devil's Kitchen.'

It's hardly the waters for a row boat or pedalo, is it?' Beer conjectured.

The boys looked at each other.

'When was this, did they say?' Cliff asked.

'Weeks back.'

With that each of them closely inspected the craft, as well as the cave itself, hoping to discover something that could tell them more. A fair length of well used rope lay coiled in the boat along with a crumpled up tatty supermarket carrier bag, stuffed under the rear seat. As he eased it out Beer became conscious that inside it was something substantial. Jago suggested it was the sort of bag fishermen often put their catch in. Beer had to agree it did smell a bit fishy.

'What have we here?' he offered, extracting the yellow handle, then blade of a Stanley handsaw, wet and coated with rust.

'There are more caves round the south coast; but we'd only make them by boat, more substantial than this one.'

'Maybe the RIB in the Dive Shed,' Beer ventured half-heartedly.

'Sure,' Cliff said distracted by the discovery of a hessian sack, full of rocks shoved under the boat's hull.

'Isn't that odd? I could understand it if the dingy needed an anchor, but a handsaw? After all the craft's made of plastic not wood.'

'Beer, you grab the saw and bag. If you're ready Jago, run us back up and I'll get the pint in I owe you.'

Beer delivered a most unnatural cough.

'Not forgetting you Beer, yours a lemonade, right?' laughingly Cliff volunteered.

The Marisco Tavern, in many ways, is much like any traditional pub but unique however, in retaining a sense of other worldliness, steeped in island history and its maritime past. It's hard to say what makes it feel so different but all would agree it does. It's not so much a home for the island boozers, but more a convivial centre for all, offering both a bar and restaurant. A welcoming establishment, and the only one on the island to have lighting after the generators shut down for the day around midnight.

Many Devon villages have lost their local pub but Lundy preciously holds onto its Tavern. Unlike so many other hostelries with their low ceilings, black beams, uneven floorboards or stained carpets, drab curtains and peeling wallpaper, smoky fire, intrusive music and chattering fruit machines, which so often define the country pub, that does not describe The Marisco Tavern. Here island life plays out, visitors can dry off after experiencing Lundy's inhospitable weather, recharge and catch up on the news of the day.

They took to the upper balcony in the eaves of the bar, resembling what one might expect in a medieval great hall, albeit on a much smaller scale. The three of them made themselves at home on a long wooden table, seated amongst an array of antique life belts, heraldic banners and relics from unfortunate vessels that had found their end about Lundy. Hardly having a chance to savour their drinks, Charlotte disturbed them.

'Cliff, your office has been on the phone and they want you to call them urgently.'

Jago piped up, 'I need to shoot across the way to the shed and shift some of the stores and machinery. Thanks for the pint; if you need anything give me a shout.'

Cliff returned after no more than five minutes to find Beer slumped against a bundle of cushions, dozing.

'All too much for you?' Beer twitched, coughed and sat upright.

'Sorry Boss. I think it's the lunchtime pint.'

'I blame the late nights here in the Tavern, no matter,' Cliff mumbled before finishing his pint. 'Charlie's after trying a public appeal and wants me to front it. I need to go on the 17.15 on Friday and I aim to be back on the nine o'clock from Bideford, Wednesday. Are you okay holding the fort?'

'Sure. There are a few things I want to follow-up and I still haven't had a good nose around the island. The word's come back from Jack's mate who is a diver and knows the waters around Lundy well, that basically the man could have gone in the water almost anywhere. The currents around the island move in directions you wouldn't think, this way and that, so there's no easy answer, but at this time of year somewhere along the south west and west coast are the most likely. It seems the Bristol Channel is blessed with one of the most impressive tidal ranges in the world, and around Lundy a significant 9 metres. So, I'll take a closer look around to Shutter Point and up the west coast; after all, that's near where the sightings were.'

SIXTEEN

Cliff's sea crossing was calm and uneventful, far more so than the atmosphere that greeted him back at Bideford Nick.

'The top brass is giving me earache. Tell me you know who did it, then we'll all be able to get back to normal.' Charlie's welcoming tone was hardly unexpected but nevertheless not what Cliff had hoped for. Of course, he didn't have a clue.

'The Chief Constable wants to put out an 'All Stations Alert.' Circulating the e-fit to every force in the country.'

'It's early days Sarge, I think we should focus locally at first. I've a gut feeling he's from around here, the West Country.'

'I sure hope you're right Cliff,' Charlie shared, more irritated than certain. 'Good, I'll call the Press Office and get them on it. Make sure it goes well, I don't want to field anymore agro from upstairs.'

Cliff eyed the press warily. He was determined to be brief and share the barest of detail, whilst projecting an air of confidence.

'Good afternoon, everyone. I'm D.C. Cranford Cliff, leading this investigation. Our enquiries are progressing and focussing on identifying the body found on the island of Lundy in the past week. We are keen to discover his identity and need your valuable assistance in making a plea to the public for their help. He's a white Caucasian, around his mid to late fifties, with no distinguishing marks.'

Cliff knew full well that the body was in such a state it was hard to judge how true that was.

Hands shot up amongst the press gang, but Cliff ignored them.

'We have an artist's impression for publication which I've made available as you leave. Your assistance is very much appreciated.'

Then came the moment in proceedings when it can all go horribly wrong.

'Are there any questions?' Their frequency and speed felt as if they'd never end.

'Was he murdered?'

'We're currently keeping an open mind.'

'Has there been a murder on Lundy before?'

'No. Well, actually that's not totally true. In 1871 someone was shot dead in the pub on the island but nobody was convicted of murder.'

One female reporter asked if there were any photos she could have of the victim, his face?

'I'm afraid not, not at this stage.'

She immediately ventured, 'Was his face disfigured?'

Cliff replied, 'We have the Forensic Artist's facial reconstruction as I said,' and accepted another question.

'What was it like when you first saw him?'

Cliff considered for a moment then professed, 'I'm not afraid of seeing death, but murder, that's a totally different thing.' He drew breath, 'That's it. If you have any further questions, call the station. I would ask you to urge any of your readers or viewers who have information to call us on our Public Appeal Line! I can't stress enough that we urgently need to identify this man; someone out there knows who he is. Thank you all!'

The regional television news that night began with the startling lead, 'Police hunt for this man. Body found on Lundy,' while the North Devon Journal printed whatever the police wanted. Conrad was well on board, busily briefing colleagues within the media. Each brought in scores of calls to the already stretched team. Fellow officers in Barnstaple were charged to initially handle the growing influx and prioritise the calls. By now, it had gone nationwide, and reporters were becoming directly engaged in following up contacts, prompting all manner of news stories; 'Mystery Body on Lundy,' 'Man found dead on island,' 'Unknown naked corpse…'

By the end of the first week of coverage, the police had checked out ninety reports. One concerned a middle-aged Dorset man who'd walked out on his wife, but after several enquiries it was found he'd left her for another woman. Still another man was said to be causing problems in a pub in Ilfracombe pushing drugs, but hadn't been seen since a brawl. So, it continued, the massive task of dealing with the inundation of well-meaning and troublesome members of the public, some claiming they knew the man proved to be a challenge the North Devon Constabulary were ill-prepared for.

Cliff knew full well that when you get a lot of calls in response to an appeal like this, you are never sure whether the information you receive is crucial and key to investigations. With so many, the risk is that vital information can get lost.

Several callers asked for details of the murder, offering no explanation why, while another suggested that the dead man knew the killer, reasoning that's how it nearly always was in crime movies.

Finally, it appeared the public appeal was paying off. A young woman rang the police late one evening; getting home from work, she had sat down and over supper browsed the paper. Seeing the artist's impression, she was convinced she knew the man and phoned the police. The woman worked behind the bar of a village pub on the outskirts of Newquay, which Clarence regularly frequented. The police had taken scores of statements but to date, hers was the most promising. She was absolutely sure it was him and subsequently the landlord confirmed the likeness of the drawing to the local bobby.

The regional papers announced that the police were closer to finding the murderer, but if asked, a police spokesperson would have had to state they weren't, and had never publicly described it as a murder.

The woman's report seemed to correlate with a call to Newquay Police Station, the day prior, from a security company that claimed one of their guards had missed his shifts over the past week. They had tried to contact him, even calling round to his address but without success, adding it was completely out of character. They wondered if the police could make some enquiries, maybe contacting Treliske Hospital. When the duty officer asked for the employee's details, they noted it was one, Clarence Nancekivell of Wesley Road, Crantock, Newquay. They assured the caller they would look into it and pass it onto their colleagues in North Devon.

Thank God, the hunt to identify the man had seemingly reaped a reward.

Andrew Maunder eventually got put through to the barmaid of the Towan Arms after explaining to its busy landlord the significance of his call.

'What do you want to know about him?' the barmaid answered.

'Whatever you can tell me?' Andrew said.

Reassuring that he wouldn't disclose her identity, Andrew added, 'Do you have another first name you'd like me to use instead?'

She considered for a moment, then uttered, 'Lu!'

Lu slid a cigarette from the packet. Lighting it she took a long drag, then resting it in an ashtray, exhaled before starting to talk about Clarence. Andrew began frantically scribbling in his note pad. Whilst in reality he was writing for The Journal, in his mind he had now risen to the giddy heights of lead reporter for The Telegraph. Although a vivid imagination can be a wonderful gift, it can at times prove confusing.

Unlike public houses in our big towns and cities where it is possible to remain anonymous, village pubs are quite different, offering more of a community atmosphere where everyone knows everyone, and also their business. Here's the place where gossip, rumours, casual comments and revelations can often be one of the same and Lu didn't miss out on any of it.

The Journal's dramatic news story broke on the front of the paper:-

The man whose body was found naked on the rocks beside the Landing Beach on Lundy has been identified as living in Crantock, on the outskirts of Newquay.

Previously the North Devon Coroner had adjourned the inquest as there was no evidence as to who the man was and how he came to be found on the rocks. The initial medical evidence, which detailed the body's many injuries, was insufficient to account for how the body ended up in the sea. The Coroner stated,

'I do not intend to close the inquest until the police have had a chance to identify the man...'

Now The Journal can disclose that the man has been identified by the police as Clarence Nancekivell of Wesley Close, Newquay.

A footnote accompanied the piece directing the reader to page 3 of the paper and an exclusive interview with someone who knew him well.

'I've spoken with Conrad at the Journal,' Charlie's voice hardly fully expressed his annoyance, 'and reminded him we had a deal, to tell us anything he had and run it past us before going to print.'

'And what did he say?' Cliff was equally frustrated but not surprised.

'Not much. Just he thought he'd give the young lad his head and see what he came up with. He hadn't realised we hadn't interviewed the lass.'

'Well, I've spoken to her on the phone but need to get her in,' Cliff admitted somewhat sheepishly, thinking there was no way he was going to be out-witted again, least of all by some jumped-up paper boy.

SEVENTEEN

'We have a name. All we've got to do now is confirm that he's our man.'

Cliff had assembled a small group of officers in Barnstaple station, briefing them on their course of action.

'Let's track his movements over say, the past five weeks. Did he use the train, a bus, a taxi? Did he have his own car, if so, check local roadside cameras, the units on the Atlantic trunk road. Also, any parking tickets and sightings in local car parks, their videos. We've got to get to know our man. Find out what interests he had, he must have done something other than drink down his local - hobbies, clubs, activities – how did he spend his time?

'My interview with the barmaid leads me to believe that if he didn't have family locally, there was someone he was, or had been, close to. She didn't know who or where but had the impression they were nearby, find out who. She also was sure that before working in Newquay he'd had a job down in Plymouth. Find out who and what if anything, they know about him? Jack's talking with the security firm to see what we can learn there. I want you,' he pointed to a middle-aged female officer, 'to liaise with Newquay. They're undertaking a door to door on Wesley Road; contrary to the press there is no Close. Let's see what they come up with?' He scrutinised the gathering.

'We have a name but we've got to find out who he was and if he is our man.' Cliff gauged their reaction.

'It's one hell of a task, let's get on it!'

Strolling beside Bideford's quay, he paused, noticing the Oldenburg peaceful and moored alongside. Calm and silent the River Torridge made its way beneath the old bridge, journeying by the reed beds, under the town's massive new concrete bridge to finally join the Taw and on to the open sea. The distinctive ocean smell caused Cliff to recall his youth and the horrendous fishing trips with his father for mackerel off Southend, and his bouts of sea sickness and nausea.

Noticing the Lundy Shore Office portacabin, nestled between the river and the park, Cliff decided it was worth following up the enquiry concerning the mystery visitor, believing this could well be Clarence. After introductions, the young woman called out to Frank in the back office.

'Well, that's a rare coincidence but I've just this minute sent a message to your colleague, Detective Beer, isn't it?'

If anything was meant to be, Cliff thought to himself, dropping in on the office was.

'So, were you able to find anything out?'

The man scurried to retrieve a copy of the fax. 'Shall I summarise what I said?' he looked at Cliff expectantly.

'Sure, and I'll take a copy.'

'Well basically, the man sailed on Friday, 26th October from Bideford, here. He bought a day return but never made it back. Lyn here particularly remembers John Smith as being a polite young Welsh man; we don't get too many of those.'

Cliff interrupted him before he had a chance to chuckle.

'When you say young, how young?'

'You can ask her. Lyn?'

She turned, facing the men and, having overheard what was said, 'Early twenties, twenty-five perhaps, not much older.'

'Right, that's been helpful, thanks,' Cliff said more confused than before.

'Shall I read you the rest?' Frank said a bit put out.

Cliff, still trying to unravel the puzzle grunted.

'While looking, we discovered another passenger never returned; it's really quite unusual. Also, strange that we didn't spot it before, that's where our new computer booking system should help in the future. He travelled out to the island on the 23rd October, Tuesday, and was booked for his return sailing on October 30th but never made it, nor since according to our ticket records.'

'And the man?' Cliff pronounced. 'Who was he?'

'Yes, we had to post the tickets to him. He had a Cornwall postcode, TR9, Newquay. A Mr Clarence Nancekivell.'

Cliff's heart skipped a beat or two.

'And the young man, the Welsh chap any information on him?'

'I'm afraid not. I hope that's helpful?'

'You don't know how much.'

As he headed back to the station along the quay, only one thing was on his mind – *now it's two missing men?*

The mouth-watering aroma emanating from a nearby chippy proved too tempting to resist. Cliff's nose was well trained to detect what, for him, had over the past years become part of his staple diet. As he relished each fatty, vinegared chip he still was unable to ignore the fact that this case was proving more complicated than he first had hoped.

A nearby newsagent had his news board propped outside on the pavement, declaring to the world '*Murder on Lundy.*' Thankfully Cliff hadn't noticed; he was too busy enjoying his chips!

EIGHTEEN

Mindful of the sightings on the island over the past weeks, Beer struck out from the village south west, making for Benjamin's Chair and beyond to the island's southernmost point. The weather was kind with no fog and any low-lying cloud had held off for him. The sight of the Devil's Limekiln blew him away with its vast natural pit and near vertical walls plunging to the ocean. From here he could look across to Great Shutter Rock, said to be thrown out to sea by the Devil himself; for this is where he brews his storms! He took the west coast trail north, past Montagu Steps, Pilot's Quay and onward to the impressive Old Light.

These police have come creating havoc, overturning islanders' lives; delving, questioning, doubting, not giving us a moment to ourselves. There's been no let-up in it. Clearly no good will ever come of it. They should accept what's happened, the accident and leave us in peace, to return to our old ways.

Beer left the cemetery beside the Old Light behind giving little thought to the many islanders buried there having breathed their last. The truth is, many leave this life not knowing to where they are going, he thought. Ackland's Moor lay before him, its tiny, rough airstrip stretched insignificantly angled across the island. For a moment he puzzled how challenging a landing would be in a light aircraft considering the incline, its substantial stone wall at one end and the many free roaming sheep. Beer knew other aircraft had found landing difficult but that was during the war.

He ventured further north, hugging the coast and lofty cliffs, the going easy over grassy fields. Coming upon the remote Battery, the one-time fog signal station, he descended to the ruined granite officers' houses and below to the gun emplacement housing the cannons. From here Beer looked out across the ceaseless Atlantic, stretching as far as America, and considered the grandeur and solitude of this island world and what a special place this was.

One of them has gone, back to the mainland but the other, he was still here, the young inexperienced one. Trying to find something out, poking around where he's not wanted, searching... but for what? I say again, no good will come of it – only upheaval, hurt, distrust and hate.

He pressed on beyond the Quarter Wall, keeping in sight a line of rocky turrets and wild cliffs into an area known as Earthquake. Here, great fissures cut deep scars into the coastline. He transversed the marshy Punchbowl Valley, its freshwater stream, and continued to the granite formations known as The Cheese, overlooking Jenny's Cove. Beer recalled it was somewhere near this point where Di, the Bird Warden, talked with a hooded man, an outsider, as he headed back from the north. Hiking east, Beer crossed the island by Halfway Wall, here the way became harder over rough ground covered in dense heather and gorse and, in parts, bog until he reached the track, the so called 'main road' which traced the island's spine. By now he was sweating. Tugging at his waterproof jacket he unzipped the front to benefit from the cool breeze. Making his way south, passing close to groups of grazing ponies, Beer strode out until the disused Old Light once again dominated the skyline. Crossing, this time west, he was drawn to the light and the lone Stoneycroft Cottage, tucked close to the cemetery at Beacon Hill. Here Douglas had overheard the arguments as he worked on the dry-stone walls.

He is here yet again. Now near, close to me, will he never give up? Go and leave us alone. Leave the questions unanswered, they're not important. Things happen, mistakes are made, that's life and for that matter, death. No one needs to be blamed for we're all guilty, just some more so than others. We need to move on; life is too fragile to worry about it. It's hardly surprising some become angry with it all, and lose control. It's past, it's history.

From Beacon Hill he passed Parson's Well, close to the place where Nigel, on that dark night fell upon what he took to be a tall old man heading south towards the village and church. Beer continued skirting the Tent Field and onward to the church.

When Beer set out, he had no more a thought than to enjoy and discover the island and its raw beauty. But subconsciously he did have another purpose in mind; to find out what they didn't know by stepping back in time to where the man had been seen, and learn what may have happened to him before he ended up in the sea, dead.

By now the pale sun was sinking low in the sky, a sign of the shortening days and winter, and Beer was aware of the emerging weather as dark clouds gathered on the horizon. Summer and autumn had moved on for another year and taken with them the calm blue skies and brilliant yellow sunshine. For Lundy, the winter offered days of comparative isolation. Warm winds driven off course battled against the freezing easterlies from Siberia, and the unhindered turbulent Atlantic gales from Canada, stirring up the barrelling seas. The island's birds were long gone, flying out to sea and south as Lundy, at one with the elements, braced itself awaiting the first storm.

Late that same afternoon, an early winter storm brought the first dusting of snow to much of the Devon countryside and parts of the Westcountry. Falling temperatures promised overnight frost and ice. The long days of summer seemed a world away.

At his cottage in Appledore, Cliff was settling down to his evening meal in front of the telly when his house phone rang. It was Doreen at the station.

'There's been an accident, Beer's hurt, the exact details are fuzzy but he's been airlifted to Barnstaple Hospital and is in Resus!'

Despite Cliff's questioning, there was little more she could add and was unclear about the seriousness of his injuries. 'Charlie is on his way but was certain you would want to know.'

NINETEEN

Just as Doreen was about to ring off, she cautioned Cliff,

'Be careful the roads are treacherous and a squad car just radioed in, the B3236 Churchill Way near you is blocked with a broken-down lorry; take care Cliff.'

As darkness had fallen on the surrounding countryside the snow had increased and the temperature plummeted, more than Cliff had appreciated. All now hurried home early to avoid the threatening blizzard. He noticed the roofs of nearby cottages covered in a white kind of icing and a silence hung in the freezing air. He thought the scene reminded him of Christmas.

As if second nature, Cliff decided he'd head back into town south on the Torridge Road, then onto Barnstaple. Nearing Long Lane, he could see the snow was getting much thicker and decided on a more sheltered route inland onto Diddywell Road, past Northam, and on into Bideford. Initially, it didn't seem too bad but quickly, as the road narrowed, the going became more hazardous. The glare from his headlights in the snow spattered windscreen made the going even harder. As his pool car hit a patch of ice, Cliff tightened his grip on the steering wheel, frantically manoeuvring to keep control trying to avoid a lengthy stone wall to the side of the road. Skidding, the Vauxhall Cavalier careered on, ploughing through snow laden bushes before coming to rest, its bonnet rammed against a telegraph pole. With the engine groaning, the dying vehicle's lights failed, returning his world to semi-darkness. Cliff attempted to bring the engine back to life, pumping the throttle, but it was no good. Surprisingly the impact had caused his driver's door to swing open as if inviting him to get out. A smell of petrol greeted him as he inspected the damage.

'Shit! Just what I didn't need,' he exclaimed aloud, hot breath teeming from his mouth as he slapped his hands together and climbed around the front of the car.

Hell! He thought then smiled, comforted to know that at least he wasn't hurt. Cliff plunged his numb hands into the undergrowth attempting to steady himself as he picked his way back to the road. Artic wear, bobble hat, gloves and boots would have been sensible; instead, Cliff pulled up the collar of his well-worn donkey jacket and hoped his old suede shoes were still water tight. A fine dusting of snow swirled in the breeze, highlighted by a cold white moon which cast a pale light into the freezing bleakness.

'Where's a passing car when you need one,' he asked himself aloud.

A winter helicopter flight comes with additional challenges for the crew of the Air Ambulance. The proportion and height of the cloud ceiling, along with the position of the zero-degree isotherm needed to be checked ahead of take-off to avoid icing. There are always risks in any flight but these can dramatically increase with bad weather – snow, winds and loss of visibility; all presenting a challenging test without also having to undertake a sea crossing.

Fortunately, Lundy was clear, avoiding any threat of lifting snow clouds from the chopper's downwash. Following a full recce of potential landing sites, the helicopter put down and, in no time, the doctor and paramedic had assessed P.C. Beer and were loading him aboard, secured on a scoop stretcher. Within 20 minutes, he was being wheeled into The North Devon District Hospital in Barnstaple.

The Resus staff received a briefing from the Air Ambulance medics as they handed Beer over to the team. The hospital's consultant on duty gave his instructions.

'We need to stay focussed, checking for possible life changing injuries.'

Along with monitoring Beer's temperature and heart rate, an initial assessment was carried out of external injuries.

'The patient has sustained injuries to his head and his right side.' the consultant indicated. 'We need to check for spinal, neck and any hidden internal injuries, especially about his head.'

Directing one of the junior doctors, he said, 'Can we order a trauma CT Scan and let radiology know we are coming?'

At this point in time, Beer was drifting in and out of consciousness, experiencing spasms of pain which, with the administration of a powerful painkiller, eased.

Some ninety minutes later, when Beer was conscious, the consultant updated him.

'It's good news; the imaging from the scan indicates there is no bleed on your brain or, for that matter, injury to your pelvis or spine. Amazing after such a fall. You have a fractured collar bone with what appears to be a detached muscle and torn tendons, as well as four broken ribs. And we've cleaned your head wounds, gluing you up. When you were admitted, you exhibited lapses of consciousness, that's why our nurse carried out some basic exercises with you, getting you to squeeze their hand and checked your nervous system as well as your vision; you may recall?' Beer looked vacant.

He then threw Beer by asking him the obvious, 'What day is it… and the year?'

Beer replied without hesitation.

'That's fine,' the consultant assured him.

'All being well, you'll be on your way in the next 48 hours, however your arm will be strapped and you'll need to take Oramorph every 4 hours. It's imperative you take it easy; no more falls. It's going to take 8 to 10 weeks to heal, maybe longer. You've been a very fortunate man, the outcome could have been far worse. Can I commend to you not to push your luck in the future,' and with that, the doctor briefly smiled.

TWENTY

'How did the journey go?' Charlie pressed Cliff upon his eventual arrival at the hospital's reception.

'Damn awful!'

'It's deadly out there.' Charlie conceded.

'Well, I'm afraid I've smashed the pool car getting here.'

Charlie squared up to him, admitting, 'It was never the best. It ran rough as anything, was often a pig to start and then bugger me, stalled when you were driving it. We've needed a new one for ages.'

Charlie hesitated looking confused. 'So, how did you get here?'

'I was lucky. Across the road from where I crashed was a grand old house, the only property around. The folks were in and once I explained to them what had happened and why I needed to get to the hospital, the old boy got his tractor out of the shed. We retrieved the car to his yard, then he ran me in his lumbering old Massey through the narrow lanes, dodging the half-covered parked cars, to

Northam. The Nick had radioed ahead to a patrol car which met us and, with blues and twos, rushed me here. Bloody lucky really.'

Charlie murmured an acknowledgement.

'How's the boy doing?' Cliff sounded more than just concerned. 'It was my decision to leave him on the island on his own. I'm responsible. We need to find out exactly what happened.'

'Well, it turns out that after all he's yet another stubborn sod,' Charlie insisted.

Having shared the doctor's verdict with Cliff, Charlie declared he needed to get back, adding, 'I'm certain he'll want to see you and I suspect you may have a few questions for him.'

'What on earth was he up to?'

'He'll tell you and it makes an interesting story,' Charlie pronounced with more than a twinkle in his eye.

'Oh, by the way, his ma and pa are in there with him, they've been here the past hour. Now tell me what do you think of the island?'

Cliff took a moment. 'I've never been anywhere like it before. I'll tell you what, although I've only been over there a few days, it's certainly weird being back here on the mainland.'

Cliff strode confidently along the baking hot hospital corridors, determined to do his utmost to remain positive. As he climbed the stairs to the appropriate floor, staff, adorned in regulation uniforms, joined him, their official name badges declaring their status and roles. A young attractive woman in Levi's and a jet black jumper over a white blouse trotted down past him, her I.D. on her neck lanyard swinging in time to the clicking of her heels on the tiled steps. A tall elderly man with thinning grey hair, combed to disguise his balding patch, bumped into Cliff on the second flight.

'Oops! Forgive me.'

As Cliff turned to acknowledge him, he noticed the fellow's gleaming white dog collar.

'Sorry Father, I was preoccupied, not thinking about where I was going.' Cliff admitted.

'I suspect many of us are preoccupied wondering that,' he replied and offered a broad beam exposing rows of equally gleaming white teeth, tinged with just a hint of nicotine. With that the man of God swaggered off, disappearing Cliff assumed, to another unsuspecting encounter.

A young ward nurse cast a cursory glance over Cliff's warrant card and proceeded to direct him to a side room, Beer's temporary residence. Through the half-glazed door, Cliff could clearly see the lad was wired and piped to all manner of machines. At his bedside, Cliff assumed, were his parents. He entered, exchanged glances with them and instantly felt a chill descend even before he spoke. He smiled as he introduced himself but no smiles were returned. Cliff could see a steely glint in the mother's eyes.

'We were just going detective,' the old father said, 'we'll leave you to chat to our boy who seems to have narrowly avoided disaster.'

'This time!' the mother added scornfully, shooting a glance at Cliff, which Cliff refused to acknowledge.

With their going, Beer mumbled something, it was hardly coherent to Cliff; probably as a result of the drugs Cliff thought.

Seeing a look of apprehension in Cliff's face, Beer attempted to share again, 'It's weird waking in a hospital bed.'

Cliff considered, *not half as weird as not waking at all.*

Beer spoke again, 'When can I…?' his voice trailing off.

'Do you want a drink?' Cliff proposed as he lifted the jug on the bedside unit. Beer nodded and having taken a gulp or two of the lukewarm water, tried again, his voice more strident above the noise of the various machines.

'Do you know, when I can leave?'

'Nope,' Cliff said, 'just one thing at a time old son. Tell me what happened, how, for goodness sake, did you end up here?'

To Cliff, Beer's reaction seemed to be that of a man more confused than unwilling to tell, endeavouring to clearly grasp the restless voices in his head.

'It's a bit of a blur,' Beer admitted, taking another drink. 'I walked the island as I said I would, well, the southern part of it, and that went fine although I didn't discover anything new. Then Charlotte had a call, from our jeweller in town. I called him back. He explained they'd been able to track down the watch…'

Cliff could see Beer was beginning to struggle, 'And?'

'And he'd found out what happened to it.'

'Which was?' Cliff said trying to maintain Beer's attention.

'Oh yes. It had been supplied to an Omega approved retailer in Cornwall ... Truro.'

'Who?'

'Yes, something like Speers, he gave me their telephone number.'

The silence returned and Cliff was endeavouring to cope with it.

'You said the jewellers in Truro?'

'Mmm!'

Beer appeared in some degree of discomfort.

'Are you okay?'

'Yes, just trying to remember.'

Another minute passed. 'The store searched their records and called me back saying, the Omega was taken into stock in the mid-seventies.'

Beer looked in pain. Cliff gave him time.

Then it came tumbling out, 'It was sold in May 1978 to Mrs Grace Nancekivell...'

'Brilliant! That's our man, or his wife anyway!' Cliff interjected; then he reflected, 'but that doesn't explain your accident, or what happened to you. Charlie tells me it's an impressive story.'

'I was about to tell you. Charlotte was in the office and overheard me as I repeated the message from the jeweller. She told me afterwards how Francesca West, when she first came to the island had shared about her earlier life, living, or perhaps working, somewhere near Truro. Charlotte wondered if she may be familiar with the family, after all Nancekivell is a common Cornish name. There was only one thing for it. I headed back up to Stoneycroft, this time to have a chat to Francesca. When

131

I explained to her why I'd come she initially seemed odd, feisty, hurt that I had a notion she was in some way involved with it. I realised I'd made a big mistake and should have kept my mouth shut. In an attempt to appease her, I told her that I was just after her advice and that seemed to *smooth the waters.* It was then that we heard an odd noise from above, followed by a crash outside. Even in the brief time I was with her the wind had picked up, buffeting against the little cottage. A number of slates had slid from the cottage roof and lay half broken on the ground. Francesca became anxious that, should the wind get stronger, more would become loose and if it rained the water would come through the ceiling and damage her paintings. In an attempt to appease her, I offered to refit them if she had a ladder. The well weathered wooden ladder appeared sound, or so I thought, and balancing rather precariously, I began to slide half broken slates back into place. I don't know exactly what happened but the next I knew, I was tumbling to the ground, and that's the last I can remember.'

'Some days nothing goes right,' Cliff said.

A knock on the door and, as it opened, the boy's concentration became distracted. A tall nurse, sporting long dark hair which kissed her broad shoulders, entered. Beer was taken with the woman's pretty face and warm smile while Cliff, impressed by her long black stockinged legs, slender waist, narrow hips and shapely athletic form, waited to observe her next move. She sidled to Beer's bedside, close enough for him to admire her large pleasingly sky-blue eyes. She proceeded to check the various bits of paraphernalia and monitors connected to the lad before enthusiastically confirming;

'You're doing well,' smiled, then, far too soon, left closing the door behind her.

Cliff couldn't remember in all his many years of visiting hospitals coming across such a pleasing offering from our beloved National Health Service.

The corridors were now busy, alive with activity, as occupied trolleys journeyed to their new homes and medical staff scurried to their stations. The chilled chlorine free air hit Cliff's senses as he departed this medical sanctuary.

TWENTY ONE

After several attempts that evening Andrew Maunder finally got through to Cliff on his home phone. He knew full well that when he did get hold of him, the reception would be far from cordial, but he wasn't expecting such an outburst.

'I wanted to explain and…'

'Explain! We had an agreement and you broke it, what's to explain?'

Andrew was unsure whether Cliff was usually like this or just having a bad day; he hardly knew him well enough to judge.

'I didn't think what I wrote would create any problems because…'

And before he could finish his sentence, Cliff burst in 'And that about sums it up, you didn't think did you?'

A pregnant silence lingered on the line, perhaps creating an opportunity to start again Andrew thought.

'I was wrong and I apologise, sincerely.'

Only a few words but just enough to defuse the moment.

'Right.' Cliff said, 'so where do we go from here?'

'Firstly,' Andrew continued, 'I wanted to say how sorry I was to hear about P.C. Beer and hope it's not serious. I liked and respected him. He was a great help during my stay on Lundy. I need to share something with you.'

Andrew got no reaction from Cliff.

'Did you hear me?' Still no response, 'are you there?'

Suddenly Cliff came back on. 'Sorry, I could smell my supper in the oven, or rather a burnt remnant of it. Say again.'

'I wanted you to hear my interview with one of the islanders.'

'You recorded it?' Cliff surmised, more than a little surprised.

'Yes, obviously, with their written agreement.' Andrew proudly confirmed.

'I spoke with several others but having listened to their interviews I doubt what they said is of any great importance. I'll obviously copy you my recordings but however, this one, I couldn't stop her talking. Towards the end of the interview, she asked me to stop recording but by mistake I left it on. The whole interview was twenty-six minutes, nevertheless in my opinion, the last four minute extract that I'll play to you now, I believe is the most significant to your investigations, that's what I think.'

'Significant,' Cliff echoed.

'Yes, it might well be, see what you think and decide one way or the other.'

Cliff got Andrew to play it twice over the phone to him.

'Of course, you recognise who it is?' Andrew explored.

'Can you make me a copy of your whole interview with her and get it to the station by first thing tomorrow? I think you've got something alright, and yes, I know who it is. This remains our secret until I tell you otherwise. Did you catch up with the bird woman who was on your boat?'

'No, I think she must have headed back.'

'And how did you get my home number?'

A contrite Andrew replied, 'From Conrad, Charlie gave it to him, wasn't that okay? I only want to help.'

No, what you want is the story, Cliff considered.

No sooner had Cliff put the phone down than it started to ring again. *What's he forgotten to tell me?* went through Cliff's head.

'And what else Andrew, did you forget to tell me?'

'Andrew? No, it's Charlotte. Is that Cliff?'

'Yeah, sorry I thought it might be someone else; it's good to hear from you.'

'I've been trying all day to get hold of you. How's Beer?'

'He's not too bad considering, and keen to get out of there; I can't blame him for that. Do you know Charlotte, what happened?'

'The first I knew was when a call came into the office from Francesca on the telephone line from the Old Light. I got the boys to quickly run up and check him out. I then called the emergency services. They were here in no time, and quickly a crowd gathered to see the helicopter land, far up the field near the Light, then minutes later, we watched it lift off, heading for the mainland. That's about all I know and thought it best you talk with Francesca yourself. So many folk have been asking questions on an island where little out of the ordinary happens, it's been a bit of a nightmare. When will you be back?'

'Not sure yet Charlotte, but surprisingly I'm missing the island.'

'We will still be here when you do and it will all work out okay.'

'I'm not sure about that. There's nothing okay about this one.'

Charlotte clearly heard what Cliff had said but decided for the present to ignore it.

'There's a couple of messages for you Cliff. Firstly Peter, the island's general manager is back and currently staying over in his house near Bideford, East-the-Water. He's happy to meet up and I've faxed his details through to the station. Secondly, I had a call from a recent visitor to the island; she wants to contact you urgently!'

'Who's that?'

'Hang on, I faxed her info too. Here it is – Morwenna Kitto, she's in St. Columb Major down in Cornwall. Something about trying to find the man in the picture. She sounded terribly upset. I told her that as soon as I got hold of you, I'd pass the message on.'

Even with Cliff's formidable and finely tuned detective skills, he was finding it hard to make the connection of the dead man to Lundy. Until he did, any motive, no matter how obscure, would evade him.

While such a mystery hung over the island it would remain a land hiding dark secrets.

TWENTY TWO

The man who came to the door was of average height, with a full head of black hair, tinged grey at his temples. He stared at Cliff through black framed glasses and spoke with a Northern accent,

'You must be the detective Charlotte's spoken about. I'm Peter, come on in.'

Firs Cottage looked, from the outside, much like the other Victorian dwellings in the terrace but inside it shouted loudly *bachelor*. Any anticipated fashionable cosiness had been sacrificed in favour of utilitarian furnishings, a soulless sparseness, and an oldie worldly décor which was clearly tired and very old. Cliff recognised the characteristics instantly.

'A tea?' Cliff nodded while still taking in the place.

'On your own Peter?'

'Sure,' came the reply from the kitchen, 'never had any reason not to be.'

'Right!'

'My job doesn't easily lend itself to family life. What about you? Cliff, isn't it?'

'Yes, much like you I guess.'

'So, tell me how can I help you?'

Cliff settled into an armchair which was blessed with far too many cushions, more than it or he could handle.

'As I am sure you are aware, I'm investigating the body on the island.'

'The murder?' Peter suggested.

'Yes, so it now appears. It's crucial we learn all pertinent facts about the man and I appreciate that, in your capacity as overseeing the island, you may well be able to help me with our investigations.'

Peter apologised for not being on the island to meet Cliff but explained that Head Office had insisted he attend an urgent meeting to discuss this unfortunate discovery. A kind of damage limitation exercise.

'The Trust is concerned that those involved may still be on the island and wanted to come up with a strategy on how we should handle it, as well as any adverse publicity. The public perception of the Trust is crucially important, impacting not only on our donors and supporters, but also obviously on finances. Island tourism plays a vital part in our operations, and we are yet to see what effect this will have.

'Last year was difficult for us. The wet summer and windy winter, together with access problems following the Ilfracombe Pier improvement works being delayed, put an extra strain on the island's viability. Then, as if that wasn't enough, at the beginning of this year we had the Foot and Mouth crisis. The previous year we had started to successfully market our lamb direct to the public and now we were faced with this new problem. MAFF left us in no doubt that should the island become infected, then all animals would have to be slaughtered. Our controls had to be stringent in an attempt to protect both our domestic and feral animals. Tourism was decimated here in the Westcountry, I suppose largely because this is where the first outbreak of the disease was discovered. In the worst-case scenario, the island would have been unable to trade in its current form, and its wellbeing would be threatened. As it happens, after a difficult start to this year, we've survived and now this!'

Cliff rested in the silence taking in the responsibility Peter held.

'So how do you think I can help you, Cliff?'

'To be honest I'm not totally sure. Did you recognise the man from the picture? Were you aware of anything unusual or anyone on the island behaving strangely?'

'I guess in short, no. Sure, incidents out of the ordinary occur but nothing that sticks in my mind as strange or unusual. Of course, it would be wrong to suggest that everything runs smoothly all the time - life on the island isn't like that - but nothing to suggest a murder.'

Cliff could see what he took to be a look of frustration overwhelm Peter's face.

'You must understand that although I manage the island and its affairs, I am not as close to all its inhabitants as some. Although I have a home in one of the Barton Cottages on the island, I spend half my time working here as well as visiting suppliers and contractors, or in the Berkshire office and occasionally Wiltshire.'

'What can you tell me about Francesca West?'

'Not a great deal,' he said abruptly. 'She keeps busy and productive selling from her studio and our Linhay Stores. I believe she's widely regarded as a competent and accomplished artist. In fact, that's one of hers,' Peter proudly admitted, pointing to an island landscape adorning his otherwise bare sitting room wall.

'Unlike some, she is someone who keeps herself to herself. Nothing wrong with that, but I do wonder what secrets folk like that hold. I'm not the best one to ask, Charlotte is much closer to all the islanders. Why, what makes you ask?'

'Just a passing remark, an observation. When are you next staying on the island?'

Peter leafed through his diary resting on the coffee table. 'Saturday week as things stand. Do you think you'll have solved the case by then?'

'Don't hold your breath,' was the best answer Cliff could offer.

Cliff's phone conversation with Morwenna Kitto proved to be more fruitful thankfully.

'I needed to speak with you urgently. I'm told you're working on the Lundy thing? The missing person, right? I have to know, have you identified the man, the body?'

Cliff couldn't cope with bombardment.

'Hold on. Who are you?'

'Morwenna Kitto.'

'Yes, I realise that. Where on earth is St. Columb Major…Morwenna?'

'Where you're phoning.'

'Sure, but where in Cornwall is that?'

'Near Newquay. You must have heard of Newquay.'
Cliff's dodgy ticker, which recently had been behaving, skipped a beat once again.

'Yes. Tell me why you wanted to talk?'
Morwenna started and Cliff, fixated by her account, didn't interrupt her. Being apprehensive about her partner's decision, out of the blue, to follow up someone in North Devon, Morwenna became anxious when the contact she had with him stopped. She tried to convince herself nothing was wrong; after all, he often visited mates from the shipyard in Plymouth. However, she became even more worried when he missed her birthday. In their eleven years together, he'd never missed it once. Then the bombshell. The newspaper article about the Lundy Island Mystery in the Western Morning News featured a picture which looked very much like him. She was beside herself and sufficiently disturbed to take a trip out to the island.

'And what happened, what did you discover?'

'Nothing,' she lamented, 'that's why I was desperate to talk to you.'

It wouldn't have taken a psychologist to detect the stress in her voice.

'Nothing at all?' Cliff persisted.

'After a crossing with some irritating youth who wouldn't leave me alone, on the island I was faced with silence. No one knew anything; well, that's what they'd have me believe. A few were insistent in knowing why I wanted to know, why I'd come. Maybe they thought I was a reporter or something.'

'You didn't learn anything, and you've no nagging doubts?' Cliff let his words linger over the phone line for a while.

'There was one person who seemed concerned and showed a degree of sympathy. She chatted to me over lunch in the pub.'

'Do you know who she was?'

'No. But I think she worked in the Tavern kitchen.'

TWENTY THREE

Cliff had hardly had a chance to take in what Morwenna had shared when Jack collared him.

'Clarence Nancekivell, born September 10th 1948 in a small village in mid Wales on the edge of the Brecon Beacons. Moved to the Westcountry and took up work with Westlands as an apprentice welder.'

In an instance Jack had gained Cliff's undivided attention.

'There he met Grace, three years his junior, and in 1970 they married at St John the Baptist Church, Yeovil. The following year their son Brian, was born and christened in St John's. In 1974 their second son Steven, was born and about that time they moved to Taunton, where Clarence worked for British Rail. There is little known of them until the accident.'

'Accident?' faltered Cliff.

'A car crash on the A358 Bishops Lydeard road at Pen Elm Hill. Clarence was driving in the middle of the road on a blind bend when his car was hit by an oncoming truck. The two boys were in the Metro, which was a right off - Brian in the front and Steven in the back.'

'When was this, Jack?'

'1986, the October. Clarence had been drinking but that wasn't the worst of it.'

'What do you mean?'

'Whilst Steven was shaken up and Clarence suffered broken ribs, cuts and bruising, it was the front passenger side of the vehicle that took the impact. The boy Brian died in the ambulance on the way to the hospital. He was just fifteen.'

'That's dreadful.'

'And for the family… shattering. It seems after that the family broke up and the trail went cold. Clarence next surfaces at Babcocks, in Devonport Royal Dockyard, Plymouth, where he signs the Official Secrets Act 1989. Steven disappears as does Grace.'

'We need to track down the young lad. How old would he be now?'

Jack referred to his notes. 'He was twelve at the time of the accident back in 1986, that makes him around twenty-eight.'

Jack could see Cliff was considering what, for both of them, had proved pretty revealing. As is so often the case, the more you learn about someone, the more questions you have.

'I think Jack, we need to find out more about Clarence's wife. The marriage and birth certificates should help us there and provide a clue to Steven, where he lives… perhaps in Wales? We've got to find him. Can I leave that with you? I'm down to Newquay to see this Kitto woman.'

St. Columb Major sat just a few minutes' drive off the busy A30 and as Cliff carefully manoeuvred through its narrow centre, he couldn't help but wonder if he was on a foolish wild goose chase. What he did know was, he wouldn't rest until he knew for certain, one way or the other.

In no time he felt he was starting to leave the village when he came upon Morwenna Kitto's house on Trekenning Road. It was one of a row, grey and drab looking, much like all the neighbouring properties. 'Council,' Cliff thought to himself. He mounted the steep concrete slab steps to her door, searched for a knocker, then door bell, and with none evident, rapped on its frosted glazed panel. It was promptly opened by Morwenna.

'On the dot. Was it a good run? You can never tell with the A30.'

She, this woman who had created turmoil with her claims, appeared the most unassuming, ordinary, middle-aged creature you'd bump into in the street, apologise to and go on your way thinking nothing of it. On his way driving down, Cliff had begun to form a mental picture of Morwenna Kitto, but his first task, now he had met her, was to disregard all he had assumed.

'It was quicker than I thought, I rarely come down this way.'

Morwenna seemed relatively at ease as she poured the tea which Cliff, on first glance, took to have been brewing for some time. The front room was crowded with all the memorabilia and trappings one might associate with a full, and colourful life. Sunlight streamed through the large bay window, highlighting a more than generous amount of dust.

'Where should I start?' She was clearly becoming agitated.

'Tell me about Clarence?' Cliff had decided to start with the familiar and see where it led. She handed him a photograph and Cliff had to admit to himself it looked remarkably like the artist's impression. Re-arranging herself on the brown corduroy sofa, she began.

They had first met in 1991. Morwenna was working in the office of a garage in town and Clarence was in the workshop. Over the years she had learnt more about his previous life and his marriage, the boys, and of course, the accident. In spite of her trying to convince him it was just that, an accident, he never forgave himself. It had weighed heavily on his mind throughout the entire time he and Morwenna were together living in Newquay. Clearly the accident, and death of Brian, had played a massive part in the breakdown of his marriage. Morwenna had never known his wife, nor Steven for that matter, although Clarence had tried hard to stay in touch with his son. Brian's death had driven a rift between them. Resting back into the sofa, Morwenna was clearly avoiding recalling the many painful moments they faced together.

'When Clarence discovered Steven had changed his name, he was beside himself with despair, doubting that their relationship could ever be healed.'

'How did he find out?'

'His wife. As he said at the time, she seemed to relish telling him.'

'So, are they still married?'

'Yes. He'd tried for a while to talk to her about a divorce,' Morwenna scoffed, 'but she wouldn't have it, probably knew the regular money Clarence provided would end.'

Cliff let her reflect for a while.

'That's why Clarence went to see her. That's why he wanted to go to Lundy.'

'And what was her name?'

'Grace, Grace Nancekivell.'

'And the boy Steven, his new name?'

Morwenna shrugged.

'Do you know where he lives?'

'Clarence thought from all that Grace would tell him, somewhere near the Brecon Beacons. I think he kept the boy's details in his desk.'

'Can I take a look?'

'Yes, of course.'

'What did you find out when you went to Lundy? I know when we spoke you said nothing, but has anything, anything at all come to mind?' Cliff knew he couldn't emphasise enough that any detail might be important. Morwenna said nothing but just shook her bowed head.

Long awaited inspiration came to Cliff. 'Did Clarence own a gold watch?'

She gave him an astonished look.

'Sure. An expensive one. Why?'

'Do you know what make of watch it was?'

'No. Only that his wife bought it for his 30th birthday. Why?' she persevered.

'We found a watch near the cliff tops on the island. An expensive gold watch.'

A silence of realisation descended, broken only by Morwenna's words, 'Do you think the man is Clarence?'

Cliff chose his words carefully, knowing what his conscience was leading him to say to this woman was not going to be comforting.

He looked her in the eye. 'I'm afraid I think it may well be.'

She dabbed her eyes with a tissue retrieved from her sleeve. Although Cliff hadn't been definite, he could see what he took to be a look of finality in her expression.

TWENTY FOUR

'How you doing old son? Are the nurses looking after all your needs?' Cliff dumped a bar of Cadbury's on Beer's side unit.

'I had the most dreadful of nights.' Beer complained, 'I couldn't get to sleep wrestling with the case, running it over and over in my head.'

'And what conclusion did you come to?' Cliff explored with the exhausted patient.

'That's the problem, I didn't. My head's full of unanswered questions. Having said that, I did think that if the murderer was on the island, the chances are they're still there. With us putting a temporary measure on those leaving the island, they've nowhere else to run to - prisoners. Isn't that right?'

Cliff rallied to the boy's hypothesis, only agreeing in part.

'That's if they didn't leave before we got there or are a darn good long-distance swimmer. We desperately need to get on the front foot if we're going to solve this one!

Peter Robinson told me that the Trust is concerned that a protracted investigation will be damaging to both the island and its visitor business. I'll be honest, I get that.'

Cliff proceeded to update Beer on the developments in the case, and as he did so he could see the young Constable's brain was in overdrive. He explained about the reporter's recorded interview, the meeting with Peter Robinson, which told them nothing new, and all about Morwenna Kitto. He shared about Jack's findings, including the car accident and fatality, explaining that in his mind it further supported the Kitto woman's statement.

'That reminds me, we need a written statement from you about the accident. Try not to make it sound as if you were being too stupid. Interestingly, Morwenna confirmed that Clarence had an expensive gold watch, and on that front the doc wants me to call in on him after I've seen you. Oh, and Charlotte told me to tell you that when the men are working on the roofs and it's windy, they wear hard hats in case of flying tiles and slates.' Cliff alone could see the funny side.

By now, Beer's face showed all the pain of a simpleton trying hard to keep up with the bombardment of information.

Although suspecting the lad was fast approaching overload, Cliff added, 'And Jack's checking Clarence's marriage certificate, the children's birth certificates and Steven's address, along with his name change. Whilst he could have just started to use a different surname, he may have legally changed it by registering a UK Deed Poll if he wanted to alter any official documents.'

'From what was said on the recording, surely I'd be right in assuming that they're our murderer, or at least that they're involved in some way Boss?'

'I'm afraid Beer we need more than just assumptions. Murder is a serious business.'

The lad's brow creased, but not for long. Beer's tall, black stockinged, slender and shapely nurse came in delivering a fresh jug of water and her unique warm smile. Without a word, as she left, Beer, with a degree of obvious embarrassment said, 'Thanks Lindsey.'

The doc was sitting alone in the staff restaurant. Cliff joined him and, as he did, a beaker of coffee was slid across the table towards him.

'White and no sugar if I remember rightly.'

'That's it, thanks Doc.'

After Cliff had tasted the liquid, he visibly cringed at the bitterness.

'You get used to it after nine years,' the doc kind of chuckled.

'So, what's all the cloak and dagger stuff, Doc?'

'Not at all. I wanted to see your face when I gave you the news Cliff.'

'Let it be good news. I can't cope with any more bad news at present.'

The doc frowned and launched forth. 'I was worried we'd have problems trying to tie the watch to our victim. As I believe I warned you, we're still in the early days of genetic fingerprinting. Dr Alec Jeffreys, the geneticist here in the UK involved with DNA profiling, was still developing the technology. However, I was aware of another system which had been pioneered in California which could work on more degraded genetic material, so I concluded one way or another that it was worth, in the first instance, to adopt Jeffreys methodology.

'We had endless possibilities to extract DNA from the body; his skin, hair, teeth, bones and marrow. The watch was a different and more problematical bag. To obtain genetic markers from a hard, steel like material which had been exposed to the elements possibly for many days, if not weeks, raised other problems. At best they would result in a low level 'touch match.' We knew the chances of getting a conclusive match seemed slim but decided it was worth a try. For if you were able to ID the owner of the watch, and we could positively match it to the body... hey presto!'

Cliff had sat patiently allowing the doc to prepare him to be disappointed. Cliff reconciled himself to yet another possible link and clue being lost. One step forward, two steps back so to speak.

'So, tell me the bad news.'

'We got a compelling match,' and with that the doc displayed a smugness, adding, 'how's Beer?'

'Yeah, doing okay. All being well he hopes to be out tomorrow. That's amazing news Doc, thanks.'

As Cliff inserted the key into the lock of his front door his phone started to ring. He dashed across to the handset just in time to stop his answerphone switching on.

'Hello!'

'Oh, you are there, it's Charlotte.'

His tone warmed, 'How are you?'

'Harassed!'

'Why's that?'

'I've got a couple of islanders who have tried to book tickets on the ferry and been told they can't; not without an okay from the police. I've explained it's temporary, purely while the investigation is ongoing and applies to us all, but they won't have it.'

'Why do they need to leave?'

'That's the thing, they won't say. I've explained they need to speak to you. When are you back?'

'As things stand probably tomorrow, the office is organising a flight. I'll prepare myself for the onslaught.'

'I wanted to ask, how's Beer?'

'You'll be able to see for yourself, he's insisting on coming back with me tomorrow. Don't worry we'll handle the uprising.'

Her parting words caught an exhausted Cliff off guard.

'Keep safe Cliff, I can't wait to see you.'

Part of him considered her sentiment reflected the desperate need for help with the brewing riot on her hands, but he hoped that wasn't the only reason. It was only as he returned the phone handset that he realised he hadn't asked Charlotte who the two culprits were; now though the flashing light on his answerphone grabbed his attention.

'Hi Cliff, this is Jack. I wasn't sure if you were back in today. I've been busy and dug up something interesting, perhaps more than interesting. Steven Nancekivell, Clarence's second son, did change his name by Deed Poll in April 1988 to Steven Coles. His address then was listed in Wales as Ty Gwyn, Myddfai, near Llandovery,

155

Carmarthenshire. I'll have a go at digging up anything
else on the lad with the local boys.'

TWENTY FIVE

Cliff was silent throughout the brief flight to the island. Beer assumed he was preoccupied with the case, and in truth, what Jack had learnt about Clarence's sons had surprised him, but Cliff's mind was on other things. As they flew over the water, he glimpsed the island shrouded by the overcast sky with a singular beam of orange sunlight piercing through the clouds, and somehow, he felt reconnected. Yet a strange sense of disquiet, a sense of mystery, overwhelmed him as they approached. With the fading of the sun's last light, it seemed as though all the colour had gone from the land, as if washed away. It felt as though this was a world on its own, perhaps a world to which one might always return.

'You were lucky to get across, we've had some serious winds the past few days,' Charlotte appeared pleased to see them and particularly Cliff, Beer thought as he watched her give the old boy a swift hug. 'You look pretty good Beer, considering. I guess it could have been loads worse, we were all worried about you.

'I've got us dinner back at my place, I hope that's okay.'

The boys were more than happy to take her up on the offer.

'I'm over beyond the shop in one of the Barton Cottages.'

'Near Peter's place?' Cliff said.

'Next door. How did your meeting with him go? Tell me later.'

'Gee, that smells good,' Beer said as Charlotte opened the door.

'Good wholesome, low cholesterol food,' and with that Charlotte gave Cliff a telling smile.

It wasn't that Cliff hadn't noticed how alluring Charlotte was, he just hadn't considered her in that way. It was only now he fully appreciated how strikingly attractive she really was: her ice-blue eyes, long red hair tied back in a bun, and no make-up on her pretty freckled face, other than those burgundy lips. Her baggy sweater and jeans for anyone else would do little to enhance their appearance, but for Charlotte that didn't matter, she was naturally good looking. As a woman, Cliff was noticing her for the first time.

After a hearty meal, some wine and casual chat appraising each other of developments, the three settled into comfy armchairs in front of the fire. It wasn't long before Beer admitted he felt pretty exhausted and undoubtedly would soon be dropping off. Taking his leave, Beer headed back to his room and in spite of the chilled night air temporarily reviving his spirits, within minutes of his head hitting the pillow, he was lost to the world.

158

'How have you been these past days, Cliff?'

Charlotte trod carefully not wanting to ruin one of the rare moments they had to themselves.

'When you spend time on your own, in your own head space,' Cliff began, 'sometimes you come up with an answer. It may not be the answer you want, but you usually come up with something.'

'Right, so what did you come up with?' Charlotte asked, uncertain if it was his heart or head talking after a few drinks.

'The truth is simpler than you think.'

'Okay,' Charlotte kind of encouraged, unsure of where this was going. She had opened a door into Cliff's past which was now haunting him.

'I neglected my wife Suzanna and that's why she turned against me. In the early days we were very much in love you know…'

'Hmm.' Charlotte replied not knowing what else to say.

'I regret it now, but my behaviour and the way I ignored her didn't help. We had the most awful arguments and she turned against me you know, and I understand why. The memories of the happy times we spent together have long since gone, overshadowed by our disagreements and battles. To tell you the truth, I'd had enough of the quarrels and her total disregard for me and the pain of her leaving for another man.'

Nothing disturbed their brief moment of silence.

'There's no two ways, I failed her and look at me now, a lonely pathetic man with nothing and no-one to live for.'

Charlotte couldn't help but be moved by Cliff's rueful deliberation although she wrestled to fully understand what actually happened.

'Let me walk you back to Castle Cottage and your bed,' Charlotte proposed.

Cliff raised no objection but rose casting his eye towards the door. The inky black night greeted them both as they picked their way along the path through the village. The moon cast stark shadows between the buildings, and reflected dancing patterns upon the breaking waves far below.

'Criminals have a habit of disappearing in the darkness. But that's not so easy on an island,' Cliff grumbled.

Cliff hadn't been cared for like that for a long while and with it he began to realise what he had missed. He had struggled to understand women, but now he was struggling to understand what feelings she had for him, as well as his feelings for Charlotte.

Standing outside the cottage, Cliff could see on the distant horizon amongst the faint twinkling town lights, the lighthouses on both Bull and Hartland Points and below where he stood, the beam of Lundy's South Light. Everywhere else was in near total darkness but here on the island, the darkness was truly dark.

TWENTY SIX

Charlotte rose early the following morning. The dew hanging on the long grass soaked her wellingtons as she strolled across to the cottage. She was unsure what she would find; a hungover and exhausted Cliff still asleep or a policeman burying himself in the case. What she did find, having rapped on the door several times to no avail, was Cliff fixing breakfast to the accompaniment of a noisy boiling kettle.

'Tea or coffee?' he shouted as she entered.

'I wasn't certain you'd be awake.'

'Well, I am, tea or coffee?'

The cottage had a stale nose to it, typical of a bedroom that hadn't experienced the light of day, nor island air recently. What impressed Charlotte most was the board, now propped up covered with notes, pictures and maps all relevant to the case. She drew closer, intrigued by what was before her. Cliff had drawn links between some of the multi-coloured 'post-it' stickers and pinpointed locations on a map of the island. She stood before it mesmerised.

Cliff's mumblings broke her train of thought.

'Oh, tea's fine.'

'Sorry, too late I've made coffee.'

'Fine, whatever,' Charlotte retorted, still engrossed.

'You've spotted my case notes. I guess it's hard to miss them.'

Charlotte didn't answer him but started to unpick the puzzle.

'For some reason anything to do with computers doesn't run smoothly in my hands,' Cliff confessed. 'No sooner have I turned the thing on and it's sallying off on its own journey leaving me behind. Hence the notes.'

'It's strange you know.'

'What is?'

'In the old days this building housed the undersea communication link the island had to the mainland. All sorts of messages and information would have come through here.' Charlotte paused for a few seconds, 'Do you have a suspect yet, Cliff?'

'Not exactly, I'm keeping an open mind. One's got to ask who would benefit from his death?'

'Have you any idea what the motive might be?'

'The usual I suspect – money, sex, revenge.'

Charlotte hardly heard his answer, she was concentrating on the display before her, however she caught his question.

'I didn't ask you Charlotte, who wanted to leave?'

'Leave?' She queried. 'Oh, the island, Shirley and Polly.'

Cliff was surprised. He knew full well why Polly wanted to leave, but Shirley, they were hardly the best of mates. He changed his tack.

'Tell me about Peter, you must know him well?'

'Yes, we've been colleagues for the past four years. He leaves me to organise the practical day to day stuff while concentrating on overseeing the governance and strategic development of the island; the buildings, monuments, the farm, as well as conservation of the island and its surrounding marine environment. Of course, he's also involved with the visitors and the ferry operation. That's crucial to the island economy, the tens of thousands of visitors each year. Quite a job even when things are running smoothly.'

'Do you like him?' Cliff never had a reputation for being anything other than blunt.

'Sure. Why do you ask?'

Cliff wasn't totally certain. He felt a kind of disconnection during his meeting with Peter and wanted to test that judgement.

'I know he's your boss and of course next door so to speak, but is he easy to get on with?'

He attempted not to sound too overbearing; he wondered whether their relationship was purely professional. Charlotte sensed where this was going.

'If you want to know, there's nothing between us,' she looked at him sternly, 'and in fact, he's moving on at the end of the year.'

'Why's that?' an eager Cliff asked.

'I don't think I can say.'

Beer had suffered an uncomfortable night, fighting to accommodate a rather demanding injured body. As the boys trekked across the island towards Stoneycroft, Beer recalled something of his conversation with Francesca. He explained to Cliff it was when he mentioned finding the watch that she appeared to get jittery. Beer couldn't understand why.

Their reception at Stoneycroft was nearly as chilled as the recent cold snap. Francesca's reaction to their unexpected arrival was plain to see as she reluctantly invited them in.

'You found me out,' her eyes widened. 'A dedicated artist who fails to sell her creations,' she gestured about the room.

Countless stretched canvasses and framed works of varying sizes, along with half a dozen easels, were propped against the walls. Sketches, note pads and a plethora of artist's materials were piled and arrayed upon every level surface.

'Let's sit, shall we?' and with that Francesca gestured towards a door opposite a sink and led them into a cosy lounge.

A small cast iron log burner set before a white mantel glowed, suggesting it might be responsible for a degree of heat. As Cliff followed Francesca and Beer, he couldn't help notice a pencil portrait of someone he thought he recognised. There was something familiar about the face. Hoping his attention hadn't been obvious he joined the others, still puzzling about his discovery.

'What do you think?' she said focussing on Cliff.

'About what?' he replied feebly.

'The sketch, the one you were admiring I hope.'

'Who is it, he looked vaguely familiar?'

'Our Peter, here on the island. You've met him I believe?'

'Of course, right.'

'But that's not why you're here is it, to check out my artwork?'

Cliff acknowledged her assumption. 'I particularly wanted to hear your account of the lad's accident. What do you recall happened, Francesca?'

'As you may realise, we get more than our fair share of wild wet, windy weather here on Lundy,' she seemed amused, Cliff assumed probably by the string of 'w's she had just spouted.

'We're cocooned in our own weather system out here. The day your constable called turned out to be one of those days. There's been problems with my roof for a while and the estate's not great at getting to it, so I was hardly surprised at what happened. If he hadn't fixed it, I may well have had some of my artwork damaged.'

'I guess you were grateful?'

'Of course. I thought at first you,' she looked towards Beer, 'had nimbly leapt off the ladder. Ironically the squall blew itself out after your fall, and thank goodness, that certainly made it easier for the helicopter.'

'And the ladder, I would be keen to have a look at that.'

'It wasn't much good so I burnt it!'

Cliff couldn't help but be irritated by what he took to be Francesca's flippant attitude, and speculated how it could be that, with such a seemingly close relationship with the island's manager, her roof didn't get repaired. It was only then that Francesca seemed to fully acknowledge Beer.

'How are you now?'

Beer managed a begrudging, 'Okay… thanks.'

Cliff considered his next words carefully. 'You don't like me, the police, do you?'

'I see people like you turning up on our island, throwing their weight around as if they run the place, making demands and changes, expecting everyone to fall in line. Your manner and ways are wrong, no good for us. I came to the island as an experiment to get away from all of that. I would be happy to see the back of you as you sail to whence you came. That's my advice to you Mister Detective and it would be good if you took it.'

'How is it I have offended you? Aren't we relative strangers? What can I say, I'm simply going about my duties and, as I am sure you are aware, it's been many years that the British Police have had jurisdiction over Lundy.'

'And what are your so-called duties?' Francesca asked frustrated by the policeman's appealing tone.

'I have no intention of destroying your island world I can assure you, I'm only here to discover how the man died and why. I hope you can understand that; but if you can't, at the end of the day, it doesn't matter. I will continue to search for his murderer.'

A silence rested between them. Cliff decided to ease the atmosphere, 'Isn't it best we start again, what do you say?'

A conciliatory Francesca said, 'I'm sorry for my outburst, it's out of character.'

Cliff doubted both her apology and the description of herself.

He said, 'I find your reaction entirely understandable and can assure you again that I'll not rest until I find the person responsible.'

Again, a silence.

'I think I would like to be on my own now,' a noticeably shaken Francesca replied.

Leaving Stoneycroft, a mournful wind seemed to rise up and chase the boys as they made their way back across the fields to the village.

TWENTY SEVEN

'Last time we spoke Shirley, you refused to tell me why you wanted to know if anything was found on the island search. Now I understand you are keen to leave the island but won't say why. All in all, Shirley, you're holding onto too many secrets for my liking. Maybe you can understand why, to me, it makes you appear far from innocent?'

She sat silent across from Cliff.

'When I first met you, forgive me, but you couldn't stop talking; you told me of how Lundy was the 'Kingdom of Heaven'; you even phoned the station to report your discovery of the body. What's happened?'

She sat speechless, clearly uncomfortable.

'You seem nervous; do I make you feel nervous? Or is it that someone else makes you feel nervous and anxious? You spoke in your interview with the Journal reporter, Andrew Maunder, of being manipulated to do things you didn't want to do, things you knew were wrong. So, is that what's happening and why you want to leave?'

'Yes,' immediately came her reply.

'So, what are these things?'

'Sharing what other islanders are telling you, the police, what you've said to them and listening to the gossip that goes around the Tavern. Also, as you know, the news about the island search. They've pressurised me to keep their identity secret; it's all getting too much so I thought the easiest thing would be to get away, off the island until it all blows over.'

Her garbled explanation tumbled from her lips, but to Cliff, it made complete sense. Shirley appeared close to tears yet Cliff realised now was not the time to let up with the questioning.

'I understand everyone's weary of our questioning but that's the only way we'll find out what happened. So, Shirley, who is it? Who's exerting the pressure on you?'

A smug looking Cliff met up with Beer in the Tavern.

'I think it would be a good idea that in future we discuss the case outside, either in my cottage or whilst walking.' Beer didn't argue but was somewhat surprised.

'Are we getting close Boss?'

'Well, my lad, I think we may well be.'

Strolling towards the church Cliff updated Beer and explained how the doc, after talking with Morwenna, sourced Clarence's dentist in Newquay and his dental records.

'He's compared the deceased Oral Structure's Report and it's a perfect match; Clarence conclusively is our John Doe.'

'That could mean his wife Grace is on the island,' Beer theorised.

'Or was!' said Cliff, his mind working overtime.
'Regarding Clarence's son, Steven, Jack's got word back from the boys in Llandovery. All they have on him is a report of Steven Coles being involved in a disturbance at The Castle Hotel in the centre of Llandovery this year, on the evening of Saturday March 30th. It seems there was an altercation between Clarence Nancekivell of Newquay, Cornwall and Steven Coles of Myddfai, Carmarthenshire. This led to a fight between Huw Jones, a work colleague of Steven Coles, and Clarence Nancekivell. Jones was badly injured and both parties refused to press charges or be checked out by a doctor. Huw Jones stated he wouldn't forget the incident, warning Nancekivell to watch his back in the future. The officer cautioned the two men, and Jones specifically against his threatened reprisal. There were no eye witnesses to clarify how the fight started and the landlord, who initially called the police, was reluctant to pursue charges.' He said, 'Steven is diabetic and sometimes his behaviour was out of control, especially if he forgot to do his injections. He could get into a bit of a rage but usually nothing came of it.'

Beer pondered for a moment, 'Do you think this Huw Jones is the fellow who confronted me in the Tavern when we first arrived?' Beer faltered, 'Perhaps he's the young man Di Silva bumped into coming back from the north end of the island that day, and he could have been the man in the row boat? Who knows?' Beer concluded.

'Someone here does,' Cliff said.

TWENTY EIGHT

'Do we need to talk with Polly, after all she was the other one who wanted to get off the island, Boss?'

'I think I'll leave that one with you, after all you seem to have struck up a natural rapport with her.' Cliff enjoyed the occasional tease of his young entrusted recruit. 'I need to phone Morwenna, she'll be on edge waiting for news of Clarence. It won't be an easy conversation but I think she's more than expecting it. The vicar's over later today so let's catch up midday at the cottage.'

'How did it go Boss?'

'As expected, she took it hard. I guess all along she'd been hoping what she feared wouldn't be the truth. I explained we'd keep her up to date with developments, and I would pass on her contact details as Clarence's cohabitant to the coroner's office. Interestingly, after my visit she had searched out Clarence's Lloyds cheque book which showed he had made a bi-monthly payment to his wife, Mrs G. F. Nancekivell for £200. She also found some old scribblings Clarence had kept, referring to the car accident. Morwenna wasn't sure but thought he'd written them way back at the time of the accident hearing. Anyway, she said that she's sent them to the address on the card I left and they should be in the station in a day or two; who knows they might throw a light on what actually happened.'

Cliff paused as if checking his mental notes, 'What about your perky Polly?'

Beer was only too aware when Cliff was having a laugh at his expense. He didn't rise to the bait.

'Believe it or not what she had to say may save us a lot of messing around.'

'Really? Tell me more. She obviously made an impact and seems to have gripped her audience.' Cliff pursued to no avail.

'It seems Shirley had a very close relationship with Francesca. Not only through her weird folk lore group, but in sharing any news and gossip she overheard in the Tavern. Polly was convinced Francesca had some hold over Shirley, she didn't know what but was determined not to get sucked in as well. I told her that was for the best.'

'And?' Cliff tried a long shot with the lad.

'And what?'

'And what about her?'

'She's a sweet lass and okay, quite a looker.'

'Compared to Lindsey?'

'Go on with you, Boss.'

The pale skinned Rev. Kenneth Cleave, sporting a military bearing, wasted no time with courtesies but pitched straight into an ecclesiastical history lesson. With a confident air he launched forth at a rattling pace.

'The first Christians came to Lundy over 1,300 years ago. In the cemetery at Beacon Hill there are memorial stones dating from 500 AD. It's amazing, isn't it? And up there are the remains of Lundy's first church dating back to the 13th century. But you didn't come to see me to discuss the church's former times, although I understand detective, you are familiar with my predecessor's 19th century Sunday School building at the top of Millcombe Valley?'

With that, Beer laughed out loud, his eyes watering with joy totally ignoring Cliff's woeful glare.

Looking around the church Cliff ventured, 'It's a substantial building for a small island community,' hoping he hadn't offended.

'Some consider this dominating Victorian gothic work of piety an edifice to one imperious man's flight of fancy. Thirteen quaymen's cottages on the island were demolished to provide the stone for the building reaching towards God as it does, four square to the wind.'

'It's certainly an impressive engineering achievement,' Beer offered attempting to sound engaged.

'A venture which way back then brought financial ruin to the island's finances and one which continues to make demands. You must excuse me, a rambling old soul. But that's not why you wanted to talk is it?'

'Reverend Cleave…' Cliff started

'Forgive me Detective Cliff but on the island I'm warmly, I hope, known as KC.'

'Right, KC, what can you tell me about the church cleaner's discovery of food and a water bottle in the church, as well as finding furniture having been moved? I believe she told you and mentioned you had also noticed?'

'Exactly. Bridget is one of our most faithful servants and what she told you is true. I caught a glimpse of the man from a distance and decided, on account of the inclement weather and being aware he wasn't causing any damage, the house of the Lord should welcome all men no matter whatever their reason.'

Beer at this point, was nodding with a degree of approval.

'That's highly commendable…' and not lingering, Cliff continued his questioning.

'What can you tell me about him?'

'I was aware after a couple of days that this was no figment of our imagination. As I said, I only saw him from a distance, and not clearly in the gloom, but we did talk. He called out to me and apologised for not asking if it was alright to stay but he found no one to ask and had nowhere else to go. I told him the church existed to offer shelter, comfort and sanctuary. I asked him if he needed anything,'

'What did he say?'

'He thanked me and said no and told me he would only be staying for a few days. To be honest, rightly or wrongly, I judged him to be an honourable guest.'

'Did he have an accent?' Cliff pursued.

'No, nothing noticeable, he didn't sound Devonian.'

'His age?'

'I'd estimate forties going on fifties.'

'Anything else you can tell us vicar?' Beer attempted in earnest.

'Ah yes, I imagine he departed in a hurry because, as Bridget reminded me, he left a small holdall in the church near where he was sleeping. There was little in it so I locked it away in the vestry filing cabinet thinking he'd be back for it. Let me get it for you.'

The boys waited in anticipation unsure what to expect.

'Here it looks like something and nothing really.'

With a hint of compassion Cliff shared, 'It seems ironic that this is the same place where Clarence rested when alive as well as when he was dead.'

'I'm glad I've found you Cliff. There's been some kind of development. You need to ring the station urgently.' Charlotte's words introduced an element of mystery to the boys' otherwise mundane afternoon cuppa in The Tavern.

For the benefit of Beer, Cliff repeated his telephone conversation.

'Well, it turns out there's a crisis back at the station. A fifteen year old lass has gone missing from her home in Braunton. She was last seen yesterday afternoon heading home after school. Her form teacher said the girl appeared perfectly okay and had said she wanted to have a chat with the teacher the following morning, today, but she never came into school. She's never stayed away before overnight. They've contacted the parents of her

177

close friends but no one has seen or heard from her. Sarge thinks it's another young girl pushing boundaries, hanging out with a boy, but he equally realises it's wrong to assume that she will turn up in an hour or two. Before long, the media will be sniffing about. 'Young Girl Missing' undoubtedly has an unhealthy appeal to their readership and that's the last thing the top brass wants, the press digging around making our job twice as hard. Meanwhile, the Barnstaple Boys are retracing her steps and carrying out a neighbourhood door to door. Charlie seems to believe we're on the brink of an arrest out here on the island and the Gaffer wants him to come over to 'the rock' and wrap things up this end. Edwin believes it will act as a distraction from anything else that might hit the fan. Although Charlie knows we're not there yet, he's still intending to come over on the next boat, I suspect to be seen to be doing something useful. The trouble is you can't argue with the top brass - well you can, but it doesn't always do any good and you just might suffer the consequences... like me. Trust me, when you get that reputation, it's hard to shake it off.'

Beer noted a degree of despair in Cliff's voice.

'The other thing Charlie said was that Jack had asked him to get me to call him as soon as I could. He wouldn't tell Charlie what it was about, only that it was imperative we speak and soon.'

'Do you have any idea what that's all about Boss?'

'No idea, not a clue.'

TWENTY NINE

'Are you sitting down Cliff?'

Jack's opening words over the phone only served to raise Cliff's inquisitiveness.

'No, I'm not sitting, don't make a drama of it Jack.'

'Do you want a chair?' came in the background from Charlotte.

'Is there someone else with you, only I thought I heard another person?'

'Yes, but it's alright, you can go ahead Jack and tell me what's got you so worked up, what's so urgent?'

'Okay, so I dug up Clarence's marriage certificate and even I was surprised.'

Get to it, Cliff thought to himself.

'He married, as I said, in 1970 when he was 22 and his wife was 19; that makes her 51 now. But this is the cracker – her full name on the certificate is Grace Francesca Nancekivell and wait for it…' which was exactly what Cliff was doing, 'her maiden name was West!'

'Well bugger me,' Cliff exclaimed.

'Exactly,' Jack said.

Cliff had believed much of what Francesca had told him, but that was until now. She had been feeding him a pack of lies and now they both knew it. The first 24 hrs are the most important of all with any crime and here they were days in and only just beginning to discover why the victim, Clarence, was on the island.

'There's one last thing Jack; can you fax me a copy of the certificate; send it to Charlotte's machine, I'm right by it now.'

Charlotte looked at Cliff, her intuition leading her to believe that whatever Cliff learnt was massively significant, and a glance at the document that rolled-off her machine only confirmed as much.

'I always had my suspicions,' Beer said subsequently upon hearing the revelation.

Cliff gave him a quizzical stare, 'That's the first I've heard of it.'

'I may not have said as much.'

'Don't give me that old son,' Cliff said with a certain disdain.

Beer had been warned from the outset that Cliff wasn't the easiest of men to work alongside and he was once again appreciating the validity of the warning.

'The world's a bit like a circus.' The sincerity of Cliff's words got Beer going.

'What do you mean Boss?'

'You only have to blink and you've missed the next act.'

THIRTY

'How was the crossing, Charlie?'

'Bloody awful. We were tossed this way and that, and for the life of me, I don't know why the outfit, Devon Air Travel, ever packed up flying here from Barnstaple. Sure, it was back in the fifties but I am certain plenty can remember it. Then when I get here, the place looks like something out of a ghost movie with a thick fog hanging over the castle on top of the hill.'

'Pity,' Cliff shared. 'On a fine summer's day, they tell me the ship's crammed with hundreds of giggling tourists enjoying a flat calm crossing chased by dolphins. Of course, you know there's a helicopter flight from Hartland?'

'No!'

'Doreen booked Beer and my flight just the other day.'

'Now you tell me,' Charlie said holding back any stronger reaction on account of there being a lady present.

'It's probably done you good Sarge, and made a change from sitting behind a desk. After all you don't get out much these days, do you?'

Cliff was pushing his luck and both knew it.

'Enough of that. Who's this attractive young lady with you?'

'Sorry Sarge, I should have introduced you; this is Charlotte. Along with Peter, the island's General Manager, Charlotte keeps the island's wheels turning. She's been a tremendous help to us in liaising with the islanders and aiding our investigations while Peter's been away. Charlotte also knows every bit of the island. You may not be aware Charlie, we've had to work out of her office because the only other phone here is open to all in the Tavern.'

Charlie sensed an admiration in Cliff's voice.

'Thank you Charlotte, local support makes a huge difference to our enquiries and undoubtedly to their success. I guess you're pretty au fait with the investigation but I am sure you realise what you learn is confidential.'

Charlie offered his hand and they shook. He turned to Cliff,

'The Commissioner understands you're on top of this one Cliff and I've not told him differently.'

He hardly gave Cliff a chance to respond.

'You are, aren't you? And about to make an arrest?'

Charlotte could see a paleness in Cliff's face.

'Not just yet. All our questioning seemed fruitless, nobody admitted knowing anything or had any idea what happened. Gradually evidence has cast a light on what happened, which will allow us to find our murderer and put them away for good. Don't you worry yourself Charlie about how things are going; if I don't find them soon, then they will find me.' With that Cliff took his leave saying he needed to catch up with Beer.

'It's good to meet you Charlotte,' Charlie offered, 'and put a face to the name. I knew you had been crucial in getting our enquiries off the ground and clearly Cliff can't speak highly enough of your help. I appreciate it can't be easy having us lot landing, digging up all sorts of stuff, some of which folk might wish was left undiscovered.'

'Oh, I don't know about that but certainly it's not been an easy time.'

'How are you two getting on?' Charlotte wondered what Cliff or Beer had said. 'What's it been like working with one of our old prize possessions?' Charlie continued.

Charlotte considered Charlie's comment. Cliff had shared with her that when confronted with a difficult question, answer it with a question.

'What's Cliff really like Charlie?'

'If I told you he was a typical stubborn detective... I'd be lying. I think he sees himself as a kind of roughneck east Londoner, a hewn version of Michael Caine, without the horned-rimmed glasses. He likes to think he appears a spot mysterious, a loner in the shadows so to speak. Not everyone takes to his single-minded recalcitrant grubby methods, certainly not the top brass. I'm certain he equally finds the officialdom of the Force crippling, but by ignoring it, he nevertheless gets the results in spite of the bureaucracy. Many, back at the Nick, see him as a local hero. There's nothing wrong with that; when you've got villains, you need a hero or two.'

Charlotte wondered if Charlie had been listening too much to Cliff.

'In the whole of Devon and Cornwall we see fewer murders in a year than you can count on two hands and here, on Lundy, it's our first. That's why we need coppers like Cliff. He has an eye for detail, for spotting clues, he's shrewd with a nose for sniffing out the truth behind the lies. However…,' Charlie paused, 'I personally find his customary manner frustrating and irritating at times, and it certainly doesn't always make my job easy, anything but.'

Charlie looked at her full in the face.

'Anything else you wanted to know?'

'What about his health?'

'Health? He's old, tired and more than ready for retirement.'

'His heart?'

'I wouldn't say he's got a heart for anything or anyone anymore.' Charlie was striving to understand where she was coming from.

'No, the problem's he's experiencing with his heart, why it misses a beat causing him chest pains.'

He looked at her amazed.

'I had absolutely no idea,' a troubled Charlie replied. 'Well, he needs to get some medical advice and help urgently otherwise it could prove to be the death of him.'

Immediately he understood he could have perhaps chosen his words more carefully. It was only then that

Charlotte grasped that Cliff was battling his condition totally alone.

Over an early lunch in the Tavern the three policemen, well away from the few others present, discussed their strategy for handling their interview later that day. It was vital they got to the truth.

THIRTY ONE

Cliff led Charlie up towards Beacon Hill and the Old Light where it stood erect upon the highest part of the island, dominating the skyline. Charlie couldn't help but be impressed, its curved granite stonework sparkling in the afternoon sun. Beside it stood the Lighthouse Keeper's accommodation, equally grand in both scale and size. Situated as Lundy was at the entrance to what was once one of the busiest shipping lanes of the British Isles, the island had in the past proved a hazard to navigation. With the top of the island often obscured by low dense clouds or lingering grey fog, the light, towering 567 feet above sea level, proved over time useless and was abandoned.

They skirted the old burial ground adjacent to the Light, the resting place for Lundy's previous owners, as well as far more ancient remains, residing beneath massive hand-hewn granite slabs. To Charlie, it felt like another world; back in time. The sturdy single storey cottage of Stoneycroft sat at the end of a long grass path which ran alongside a substantial dry-stone wall. There, within a neat lawned enclosed garden, it stood alone, forlorn. A dozen or more sheep tightly huddled against the stone wall stared out across the empty moorland and open fields, waiting for a change in the weather.

Cliff, with more than a passing acquaintance with its resident, regarded it as being a place that still held many secrets. As the door of the cottage opened, Cliff immediately introduced his superior, Charlie Harris to Francesca.

'It is kind of you to see us,' Charlie intervened, proceeding cautiously with the woman knowing her welcome was unlikely to be warm.

'May we come in, and I can assure you we'll take only a few moments of your time? And please call me Charlie, I hate unnecessary formalities.'

Her eyes widened. Cliff was unclear whether it was Charlie's charming manner, apparent understanding or smart uniform, but concluded something did the trick.

'Thank you, Francesca,' Cliff said, noticing for the first time her natural beauty and her face which had no need of make-up.

They were encouraged to follow her, through the pantry cluttered with paintings and, what Charlie took to be 'tools of the trade', into her snug. Each of the men were offered a broad armchair by the window while she faced them seated on a sagging beige sofa gilded with brightly embroidered cushions. As they sat down, a fine mist of dust rose and glistened in the cool sunlight. Cliff had failed on his last visit to notice the surprising lack of photographs, family portraits either standing framed on the tables or book case, or hanging on the bare white-washed walls.

'What is it now?' Francesca addressed Charlie in a firm tone.

Charlie came back equally determined,

'Just a few loose ends, nothing more, although there is one thing I would be keen to know.'

Francesca couldn't resist the lure,

'And what's that?'

'I couldn't fail to notice as we came in, your fabulous paintings. I would love to hear about your amazing work, a real talent.'

Cliff thought Charlie had overdone it but fortunately it appeared that Francesca's pride had caused her to be oblivious to that. Apparently inspired, Francesca began.

'When moving here I became captivated by Lundy's intrinsic wild environment; it's rugged character. Over the years I've developed my own style, becoming increasingly grounded in the natural landscape, focussing on Lundy's unique weather and wonderful light as I create my compositions. I strive for my work to convey a feminine harshness focussing on the island's beauty.'

Cliff was impressed by Charlie who seemed to be re-discovering his old misplaced skill of listening.

'In many ways I'm 'old school,' being self-taught I experience a close emotional engagement with my medium.'

'Self-taught, that's amazing. When did you realise you had this natural gift, the flare which is clearly evident in your work?'

Charlie was more than able to lay it on, and thickly.

'I always loved painting and drawing as a youth and I never want to lose that love. It can at times be challenging trying to make a living in such a remote location but visitors are captivated by the island and my paintings and love momentos of their stays and are well able to pay handsomely. I also receive a steady flow of commissions thankfully.'

'And what medium do you enjoy?'

'I mostly work in oils, thick and rich, allowing me to mix them freely on the canvas creating energetic works. Maybe you'd like to buy one Charlie?'

'Yes, perhaps I can have a closer look when we get these few questions out of the way.'

'Would you like a tea or a coffee?'

'No,' Cliff said. 'Thank you all the same, but we don't want to keep you.'

With Charlie's apparent success Cliff decided to leave it to him.

'I know my detective has already checked with you but I wanted to be doubly sure we have no misunderstandings. Is it okay to call you Francesca, that is your name, isn't it?'

Charlie gave her plenty of time to respond, but to him she appeared irritated and flinched.

'I believe you seemed to take the man's death hard, yet you didn't know him, is that right?'

'Yes!'

'You didn't know him?'

'No, I didn't.'

The repeating of the question to her came unexpectedly.

'Who was he?'

'Well, we're still unsure; the body was in no great shape.'

'And you think it was an accident?'

'That's something we are keeping an open mind on.'

'Surely you don't believe he was murdered?'

Both Charlie and Cliff didn't know how much longer they could string things out for but fortunately they didn't need to; there was a knock at the door.

'More visitors?' Charlie said.

'None I was expecting,' she declared heading towards the door.

In no time Beer had followed her into the room. He handed Cliff several sheets of paper then shuffled uneasily and, as if needing to be excused said,

'Sorry to interrupt but this came through for you Boss, and it's urgent.'

The top sheet was familiar to Cliff but not the other note from the station. He read it and passed them over to Charlie. Cliff spoke.

'We now know the man's name and,' he pretended he had to recall, 'is Clarence Nancekivell. Does that name mean anything to you?'

She didn't answer him.

'Well, I would have thought it should, because according to his marriage certificate, he was your husband…Grace.'

Francesca stood, and both Cliff and Charlie wondered that if by playing out this macabre performance, they'd pushed her too far. She approached the wood-burner, opened it and taking a poker, shifted the white ash around the grate, encouraging it to fall into the ashtray. As she did, briefly a flicker of flames danced on the smoky peat blocks before dying and returning to the shadows. She pulled across the worn flag stone floor a low wooden stool and sat before the fire. Francesca didn't look at them.

'I'll ask you again, tell me about Clarence?'

She spoke with a surprising calm. 'There had been good times, but that was before the accident. After that, it was never the same.'

She closed her eyes and briefly her whole body stiffened as she recalled their time together. Soon her words took on a darker tone.

'My feelings are confused,' she smiled the same smile that had before disguised every one of her lies. 'The terrible death hung over us like a bad omen. Clarence's presence haunted us, those of us who had survived. I am plagued by memories I want to forget.'

Charlie knew full well, even after only a brief time with her, that she had so much more she was not telling. A thought lurked in the back of his mind that seemed improbable.

'So, what did you do, how did he die?'

'If you're asking, did I kill him, then the answer's an emphatic no!'

He struggled to recognise that this beguiling woman, at the very least, was a dangerous beauty but more than that, a lying bitch playing a part in this deadly charade.

'So, if not you, who?' Cliff demanded conscious of his mounting suspicions.

Francesca had sensed that sooner or later it would come to this. She could hear her heart throbbing in her ears.

192

'I am not responsible for his death. I had nothing to do with it!'

In spite of her loud protests, the others gravely doubted her.

'Who hated him enough to want him dead?'

Cliff realised it was unlikely she would tell. Francesca's cheeks flushed, then her face grimaced. What they desperately needed was the truth and an end to the lies and deception. They needed to know what happened and for the game to be over.

Charlie spoke, 'I don't know Francesca, whether you understand the seriousness of your position, the difficult situation you are in? You have deliberately wasted police time, obstructed our investigation by knowingly providing false information, perverting the course of justice. Be in no doubt dear lady, you could be prosecuted under Section 5-2 of the Criminal Law Act of 1967 and if found guilty, serve a six-month prison sentence. We are well within our rights to cart you off the island to the station, but I'm sure you wouldn't want that?'

Francesca spoke quietly appearing unmoved by Charlie's tirade.

'Even now that he is dead, he is still killing me.' She considered, 'You should be careful accusing me. Your ego to arrest someone has clouded your vision of seeing the truth and learning what actually happened, not what you want to believe happened to solve your precious case.'

THIRTY TWO

The other papers Beer passed to Cliff, referred to subsequent enquiries made by Llandovery Police. They had checked on the whereabouts of both Huw Jones and Steven Coles around the time when the body was discovered. Jones's employer confirmed he was at work throughout all of October and November, including working on Saturdays. Both Jones and his wife stated he never went away over that whole time. Huw Jones did none the less say he thought Steven Coles did go away around then, and added that he hadn't seen him for some time. Coles' neighbours said Steven went away the last week in October, they made a note because he asked them to keep an eye on his cottage. He left them no forwarding address explaining he would be away only a few days, visiting family in the West of England. He hadn't been seen since and they were beginning to get worried.

Cliff edged forward in his chair, expecting yet another lie. 'Right now, we have a lot of unanswered questions Francesca. Maybe the truth hides somewhere we've not considered. Was it Steven your son, was he involved? That would account for the sightings of a stranger on the island, a young man.'

'You know nothing of my family or our world,' she said angrily.

'And that's why we're asking you to tell us,' Charlie's manner was conciliatory. 'You see Francesca, we are faced with an enigma. We now have the mystery of another missing person, your son Steven.'

With a personality every bit as strong as Charlie's, she looked him in the face, fixing him with her penetrating glare. Fortunately, Charlie held no credence in an evil eye.

'How much longer, Francesca, are we going to pretend you don't know anything?' Charlie's voice had a power and sense of authority.

'Have you ever considered a woman might have done it? Probably not, because you coppers are men. Why not let it end with me? Agatha Christie wrote some of the best murderers are women,' she said sneering.

What they were hearing seemed totally contradictory, then they realised her game, weaving a web of confusion.

'What if I told you that the man who is responsible for the murder of your husband is with us, the police now?'

'Then you'd be lying!'

'So that makes at least two of us Francesca,' Charlie scoffed.

She steeled herself from any outburst. Charlie detected a weariness in her expression.

'I think we're about done for the present, unless there's anything else you want to share, but dear lady, you won't be surprised to know we will be back and very soon.'

He was right, she wasn't surprised.

Departing Stoneycroft, the boys crossed the old burial ground, where now pilgrims rested alongside rogues, outlaws, criminals and scoundrels, and it seemed a fitting place for Grace Francesca West to reside. A biting wind chilling every bone in their bodies, accompanied the boys as they slowly made their way down to the village, considering their next move.

THIRTY THREE

'Is it okay to use the back office?' asked Cliff as the three shivering grown men filed past Charlotte who was absorbed in despatching an order for the island stores.

'Do you want a coffee, only I've just put the kettle on, I can top it up?'

There was no second thought although Charlie commented, 'I certainly wouldn't want a local Hockings ice cream, even if you've got me one.'

Having taken in the steaming hot drinks, Charlotte pulled the door to on the policemen who seemed now to be thawing out.

'Shout if there's anything you want,' Charlotte called before getting back to her computer.

'What kind of person are we dealing with?' asked a confused Beer.

'A very troubled one,' Charlie suggested, 'and if my instincts are correct, experience tells me that often the person with the most to hide launches the first attack.'

'Well, she certainly fits that profile,' Cliff shared while supping a mug of hot coffee. 'I find her outbursts exhausting. There's something queer about the whole case. What I mean by queer is, something not right. What's with this ruddy Agatha Christie quote. She'll be into Conan Doyle before we know it. We need to go through the statements again Beer, checking for anything we've missed.'

'Right Boss,' Beer acknowledged unsure where to start.

'The problem is that the woman, who at the very least, could have stopped the incident, looks as though she's going to get away without so much as a scratch.' Charlie unsurprisingly couldn't contain his frustration. 'And the feller who should have been left alone, is washed up naked on the rocks and now lying in the morgue about to be buried in some forgotten spot.'

Cliff replied, 'My dilemma is not knowing exactly what she is guilty of,' insisting, 'I'm certain she's involved and I have no intention of letting her get away.'

'With what though?' Charlie threw in, 'That's the problem Cliff. It's one thing having your suspicions and simply another to be able to prove it.'

He knew they had not a shred of evidence against her, it was all circumstantial.

'Have you got to head back Charlie, to sort the missing girl?'

'Are you joking, Cliff? Not while we haven't got our man… or woman. No, there's unfinished business here and I want to see the end of it. Time is not on our side, we need to use it to get to the truth of what exactly happened. We need a confession.'

Charlotte had been occupied in the front office, half overhearing the men's post-mortem of their interrogation of Francesca, when her fax machine started chattering out pages. She knocked and pushed open the half-closed door, then entered. The men hardly noticed her, fully absorbed in discussion.

'What do you fellows know about empathy?' An irritated Charlotte invited. They looked vacant.

'What precisely do you mean?' a perplexed Beer shared.

'Forgive me, but from what you've said, Francesca sounds as though she's involved with her husband's murder and probably knows what happened to Steven, her son. None on the island know her well and certainly not her past life, but to my mind that makes her dangerous, someone who will stop at nothing to preserve her apparent innocence. The reason I say that, is because Francesca doesn't just like living here, the island is her whole life. I wouldn't underestimate her. I have no idea how far she'll go to stay here. She's a most determined single-minded lady, and it sounds as though you are finding this out. I am certain she'll do anything to avoid being incriminated and probably sees herself as a victim in all of this, blaming others for what's happened.'

'So Charlotte, what do you suggest?' Charlie waited for her reply.

'Somehow you have got to give her the confidence that it's safe to share what happened, and by doing so, she'll feel a release from the burden she's bearing, allowing her to finally step out from the shadows.'

'And we'll discover what really happened,' Beer proposed.

'She's fought and survived for so long, holding onto her secrets.' Cliff was now thinking out loud. 'But how are we going to get her to reveal all she's been hiding?'

'You've got to present her with a factual scenario for which you have proof, stopping her from disputing it and get her to fill in the gaps. Avoid trying to second guess what she's thinking or using deception, she's too sharp for that.'

Almost as an after-thought Charlotte added, 'And this might help,' and handed Cliff the four pages of Clarence's notebook faxed by Jack.

Cliff flicked through the pages, scanning as he did, increasingly becoming enthralled by what Clarence had written.

'Is that as captivating as it appears?' Charlie's words had the desired effect.

Cliff looked up. 'Judge for yourself,' and handed the four sheets to Charlie.

After a few minutes Charlie exclaimed, 'Bless me!'

Throughout the episode Beer remained patiently ignorant, 'Sir,' he begged.

'There you go Beer, see what you make of it.'
Charlie eased back in his chair, pensive. The lad read and re-read Clarence's words, then presumed to break the silence.

'The boy caused the accident!'

'Well, if you believe Clarence's account.' Cliff said.

'And that accounts for what Douglas heard,' Beer shared without thinking.

'Douglas who?' Charlie remarked.

'Douglas McIntyre, isn't that right?' Cliff speculated. 'So, what about him?'

Beer explained at length that Douglas had collared him that very morning, clearly agitated.

'Although he told us he couldn't hear what was being argued about at Stoneycroft, when he was rebuilding the wall, he now recalled something of what he heard shouted and he wondered if it might prove helpful. He had been listening to the news on the radio about an accident when it came back to him.'

The other two avoided the temptation to interrupt the lad's protracted divulgence and let him have his moment.

Beer coughed, clearing his throat.

'I don't know… no, I didn't know if it was relevant.'

'Don't hang it out Beer,' Cliff insisted.

'They were arguing about a car accident and he could have sworn it was two men both claiming it wasn't their own fault. That's it.'

'Bugger me and I didn't believe in coincidences,' Cliff sighed.

'I don't suppose he recognised the voices?'

'No.' Beer said.

Charlie added his two-pennyworth, 'We know who the dead man is, but not who killed him. We suspect his wife is involved up to her eyes in his murder but don't know how. Their son Brian, is dead but we're unclear who is exactly responsible for that, and the second son, Steven, well, he's missing, probably keeping out of our way. Is that it?'

Cliff couldn't help thinking Charlie's uninvited summary was unfortunately spot on.

THIRTY FOUR

'We either get Francesca to talk or find Steven,' Cliff was vocalising his thoughts. 'He is crucial if we want to find out what happened. From what she said it sounds as though he's turned against her, so maybe willing to speak to us.'

'I don't know about you but I've had it for the day and am turning in,' Charlie shared as he started for the door.

'Me too,' Beer said 'that's me done!'

Cliff looked at Charlotte, 'A night cap?'

Over a coffee, a spot too milky for Cliff's liking, the two mulled over the day.

Charlotte spoke plainly, 'When word gets out you lot suspect Francesca as being involved in her husband's death, a man the islanders never knew existed, they will turn against her and ostracise her. And she knows that.'

'But they'll not know until we arrest her.' Cliff was feeling his way.

Charlotte was definite, 'They already suspect. You must remember this is an island. Lundy's same magic and mystery that captivates islanders and visitors alike, has the power to influence both this place and its people, casting a cloak of self-preservation over this land.'

'Wow, that's heavy for this time of night,' Cliff said.

'It may be, but it's true,' Charlotte was clear. 'Here, faced with endless seas and skies, our vision of the world is not the same as many others, limited only by our imagination.'

'Right,' Cliff was more uncertain than ever. 'We need to get the killer to open up and share their story but it feels as if the truth is some way off.'

'So, what type of person is responsible?' Charlotte said.

'What do you mean?'

'Well what traits and characteristics might they show?'

Cliff considered for a moment, then theorized. 'They might appear grandiose, demonstrating a complete lack of empathy and disregard for others' emotions, a disconnection. They'd probably be reluctant to take responsibility and be impulsive and certainly manipulative, maybe by using charm and lies, remorselessly hiding behind a mask of sanity.' He waited, seeing she was envisaging something or someone.

'Do you know anyone like that?'

This utterly disarming and infectiously endearing individual uttered, 'Maybe!'

'A man?' Cliff said.

'What makes you think it's a man, Cliff?'

'Only that they usually are,' Cliff explained. 'In my years of hunting criminals and killers, it's normally a man. But I desperately need to hit the sack, tomorrow's not going to prove easy.'

She pecked him on the cheek and saw the flushed face of a man she increasingly knew. Cliff felt his chest tighten.

'You didn't say who you were thinking of?'

'No, you're right, I didn't. I guess there are aspects of those characters in all of us.'

A sense of trepidation consumed her and she shivered.

THIRTY FIVE

'Morning Sarge, how's it going?'

Charlie had told Jack to keep him updated on the Missing Person Case, and Jack's call from the station had caught Charlie in the Island Office savouring his first cuppa of the day.

'So so. What have you got?'

'We've checked the Barnstaple and community hospitals, no joy. Apparently, she always followed the same route home but no one has seen the girl, and we've nothing on the local buses and taxis. Friends haven't seen her since the end of the school day, and family and neighbours have no idea where she is. According to the school she's a solid lass, steady, reliable and sensible with no record of truancy. There's no history of mental health problems or difficulties at home. On the day of her disappearance, she acted perfectly normally, saying she'd come straight home. In the meantime, the public have got right behind our appeal with many volunteering to help search the Burrows and beaches. She appears to have vanished without a trace; I'll keep you up to speed, Charlie.'

'What's the latest?' Cliff asked, over hearing the end of the telephone conversation as he entered the office.

'Not good. What we need is an enthusiastic, shrewd boy scout with finely tuned ferreting skills to sniff her out, or better still, for her to just pop up out of the woodwork unharmed, wondering what all the fuss is about. But my fear is this one may not end well.'

'We now need to be firm and take the lead in our questioning of Francesca, Charlie.' Cliff was beginning to run through some ideas in his head.

'Does she know we're coming?' Charlie said.

'Yes. Charlotte spoke with her, offering to come along for support, but she said she'd be fine.'

On reaching the ancient granite cottage of Stoneycroft, the pair approached its rear porch door with a degree of apprehension. They were surprised at her demeanour; pleasant and accommodating. Settling in the snug, Cliff spoke first.

'I'm looking to explore with you Francesca, a possible scenario, is that okay? It would be good if you could help me paint a picture.'

Charlie was sufficiently intrigued, while Francesca just stared at Cliff, a man who she knew in the past hadn't believed a thing she'd said. Cliff didn't say another word, he let his request rest with her.

'So?' she challenged.

'The car accident and death of Brian understandably caused a huge impact on your family, and with Clarence driving a rift between yourselves and break down of your marriage. Moving to Lundy must have been a massive relief for you, and somewhere where you could safely start a new life, trying to put the past behind you. But that was not to be. Steven couldn't let it rest. The loss of his older brother in such tragic circumstances, whom he was so close to and loved, unsurprisingly drove him to become estranged from his father. Earlier this year, on the 30th March to be precise, Clarence met Steven in Wales in an attempt to rebuild their relationship, but this was met with hostility. In spite of your efforts Francesca to reconcile the two, Steven's hatred had destroyed any hope of that. He had not only grown away from Clarence but was increasingly becoming a stranger to you too. On 26th October, when Clarence was here on one of his visits to you, Steven, knowing of the visit, maybe from you, arrived on the island. Driven by the knowledge of what really happened in the car, Steven's unbalanced mind could no longer cope. For him, changing his name hadn't been enough to forget the past. Stoneycroft was the scene of a mighty argument, overheard by someone working nearby, with Clarence confronting Steven with the truth. The argument got out of hand, and a fight ensued resulting in the death of Clarence, probably from head injuries, a fatal blow to the back of Clarence's head. You see the expert pathologist opinion is that your husband was dead before he reached the water. Obviously, we don't know if it was accidental manslaughter. Maybe Steven was suffering with mental health problems to the extent he lost control, and had no intent to kill. We won't know that until we find Steven.'

Cliff paused, but not long enough for Francesca to start another game. Appealing to her better nature, he continued. 'We only want to get a picture from you as to what really happened, Francesca.'

For a moment, Cliff could have sworn Francesca's whole body was trembling.

'I wasn't there when it happened,' she spoke as if her words were to be heeded.

'They were here one minute fighting, then gone the next.'

Cliff sensed she was hesitant to continue. 'How did Steven know Clarence would be here, on the island?'

'I told him. I hoped they could make amends and settle their differences.'

'So why was Clarence here?'

'He occasionally came over, but this time was different, he wanted a divorce so he could marry his woman.'

'How did you feel about that?'

'Sad, but it would never be!'

With this Cliff felt certain they were getting nearer to the truth.

'Do you have regular contact with Steven?'

'Probably most months.'

Charlie interjected, 'So where is he now? How can we contact him, we must talk to him?'

Francesca kept silent.

'He's your son, why isn't he here?' Charlie persisted.

'You're not going to give up looking for him, are you?' Francesca understood.

Cliff interrupted her before another barrier was put in their way.

'So, tell me the truth Francesca; it's the only way you're going to escape all of this…,' he stumbled unsure how to describe it, 'and be free.'

'Steven had gone off with Clarence, ranting about the accident and how it was all his father's fault. Some half hour later he came rushing in and in a hell of a state. I'd never seen him as bad as that before. He demanded I follow him. They had continued the argument as Clarence headed back to the church. Steven, again and again, protested afterwards to me that it wasn't his fault as we ran towards the cliffs. As we approached the top he froze and told me he couldn't go any further being afraid of heights. I went to the edge and looking down saw Clarence, his face looking skyward and his twisted body sprawled over the rocks being battered by the sea. I crouched to see if I could crawl down to him but it was far too slippery on the loose rocks and shale. My whole body was shaking uncontrollably and a feeling of despair swept through me sapping any strength I had. It was then that Steven loomed over me and I saw a man I no longer knew. He appeared strange, almost possessed, lost to me. For a moment I feared what he might do. I screamed.

'Waving his arms he shouted, *'He fell, jumped, I don't know why.'*

'Then he started laughing, calling out, *'No more, never again. I meant no harm.'* I realised then there was no way I could ever know what exactly happened, it was lost in Steven's mind but that didn't matter, just having my doubts was more than enough. I don't know how long I gazed down, weeping and, for the first time in years, I remembered our times together, our happy times. I fought hard to contain the rage I felt, convinced Steven had a hand in this tragedy and it was then I realised I had been here before, many times doubting my own son.'

She took a drink of water from a glass tumbler.

Describing the exact spot she said, 'Few people hike to that place, but because of our wild currents and prevailing winds, I knew Clarence wouldn't have been laying there long. At that time, I thought it was useless telling anyone, trying to rescue the body would have been risking more lives, for no real reason.'

For a moment Francesca appeared deep in thought.

'I'm here all day long and in the winter, I hardly see a soul, just a handful of folk if I journey to the stores. I spend most of my time questioning, puzzling over my past life.'

She shook her head as her body bent forward. Looking exhausted she murmured, 'You want to believe I'm guilty, you had already made up your minds. I didn't kill Clarence,' her voice was strong and steady.

'Did you love him?' Cliff said.

Francesca's words seemed to come from afar, 'I didn't realise it before but yes, I do.'

'You mean you still love him?'

'Yes. Death is only a door. Do you know detective, what it's like to lose someone you love?'

Cliff answered 'Yes' before fully considering his answer.

'And Steven?' Charlie persuaded.

Francesca came straight back. 'The truth you want to hear may not be the truth you want.'

'What do you mean?' Cliff said, 'what truth?'

'Steven was not an innocent passenger in the car. Obsessed by the knowledge that his own actions played a major part in causing the accident, Steven's unbalanced mind became riddled with guilt. Changing his name hadn't proved enough to change the past. On Lundy Clarence confronted Steven once and for all with the truth. His fighting with Brian from the back of the car was enough to distract Clarence from his driving. As he tried to separate the two boys, Clarence lost control of the car causing the accident and the death of Steven's beloved brother and our beloved son.'

She paused in reflection. 'As a small child everyone who knew Steven loved him; there was no reason not to, but now I realise no one actually knew what Steven was truly like. They couldn't, because he didn't even know himself. I guess it's hard to when you're half crazy.'
She considered the two police officers and said,

'I think you need to leave now, don't you? I don't want any more of your questioning. As for Steven, I'm certain you'll find him soon, but I can't tell you where.'

The two men found it difficult not to be moved by her devastating account and they couldn't but feel a degree of sorrow and pity for her. Any colour had been washed from her face which was now consumed by a dispirited emptiness.

As they left, they both became conscious of Francesca's gaze following them. A refreshing sweet-smelling breeze travelled with them as they made their way back and they knew full well the dark time they had spent with her had changed everything.

THIRTY SIX

'This is the place!'

Cliff's words brought him and Charlotte to a halt. The late afternoon's supernatural sunlight filled the sky. The air was tinged with a slight winter chill which had been waiting for the day to come to an end. There was a surreal stillness which captured the island, something rarely witnessed at this time of year. Only the faint sound of breakers disturbed their thoughts.

'This is definitely the place,' Cliff stressed, 'it's the place Francesca so clearly described where Clarence had fallen.' As they crouched low, close to the edge the smell of dank undergrowth greeted them and the moist grass soaked their trousers.

'I wanted to see it for myself, see where he died.' Charlotte, by now had learnt not to question Cliff when he was engrossed, but this was an exception.

'Why?'

Cliff was not surprised by her lack of understanding.

'To see for myself and attempt to get a better sense of the woman. To try and grasp what really happened here.'

'And have you?' she asked, not in any demanding way. She patiently waited for a response.

'We must go down. There's a narrow path a little way below.'

'That's a sheep track and we're not sheep.'

'I just need to…'

'What?' she said as they skirted the cliff face together. Slipping on the wet grass, Charlotte clasped his hand even tighter. What she would give to be relaxing in her fire-side chair back in the cottage, raking the coals and glowing embers, listening to the crackling flames. But for Cliff, he sensed he just needed to be as close as he could to where Clarence had lost his life. This man, whom he never met, yet no longer seemed a stranger to him.

The cliff plunged down beneath them, way down to the ocean and rocks to where his dead body had come to rest. Clarence's actions had in some way reunited his family, albeit painfully. A light breeze whipped up a fine sea spray which wisped and foamed white on the jet black rocks below.

'Help me God; I've got to find out what happened here,' came Cliff's words of despair.

Charlotte knew Cliff to be honest and determined, but that didn't stop her finding him madly frustrating at times, and sometimes a bit of an arsehole.

'So how exactly are we going to get back up?' she said. 'I know you feel alright now but it's one heck of a climb for an old man.'

'You're with me, I'll be okay.'

'Yes, and I'm a realist.'

'And that's what pessimists say!' Cliff said, a little concerned that he may have overdone it.

Cliff looked out to sea and as he did, he tried to envisage the scene. 'Suffocated by guilt and his madness, Steven could see only one way out, the destruction of his father. In a rage he attacked the old man, needing to finally end all that haunted him about the accident. The accident that in truth, he himself had caused along with the horrendous death of his brother. Full of hatred and confusion, he tragically saw no alternative. He lashed out viciously against Clarence again and again, over-powering his father. Any innocence, any love had been destroyed by a dominating force for, as he saw it, revenge. No pleading for mercy seemed to stop Steven's assaults. Then he glimpsed his father's life fading. Whether it was a sudden urge to end it, or if some other force came to bare, a heavy blow hit Clarence on the head and then another. The mortal strikes had been delivered, and with it, Steven released Clarence to tumble down to the waiting rocks and hungry sea. Clarence's fight for life was over.

'Steven may have hardly regretted the evil death of Clarence, and Francesca knew, because of what had happened here, things would never ever be the same between them, Steven's torment would never end.'

'What are you thinking?' Charlotte asked Cliff.

'To be honest it doesn't matter what I think, that's immaterial. What matters is the truth.'

'Perhaps Francesca was trying to rescue Clarence and maybe Steven, her only remaining son?' Charlotte said.

219

'Yes, maybe, and perhaps maybe, herself. What I do know is, lies are often made up with bits of truth, and finding those bits will give us the answers we need.'

As they climbed back up Cliff's heart began to race. The long ascent had caught him off guard and now his heart was thumping hard in his chest. It suddenly felt as if it had almost stopped, sending him stumbling to the ground. He steadied himself, his hand grasping the wet grass. It was clearly painful as he took deep breaths.

'Is it your legs?' Charlotte said, hopeful that's all it was. He hesitated, trying to answer her. No words came out; his mouth dry and coarse.

Distraught Charlotte managed, 'Am I witnessing a testament to old age!'

Cliff's heart and lungs steadied as he came to terms with his feelings.

'No, my jumpy ticker I'm afraid. This is a place for those with iron wills and strong hearts.'

'I didn't think you had a heart,' and although relieved seeing the colour coming back to his face added, 'after all, you're a detective, aren't you?'

Cliff rallied, 'Do you know the average heart does three billion beats in its life-time?'

His sense of humour was returning.

'Although I've not been counting, I do know Charlotte, that you have a warped understanding of detectives.'

THIRTY SEVEN

As Cliff and Charlie entered the office they were greeted by the sound of an eager kettle and Beer's satisfied expression

'So, tell me Beer, why so smug?'

'You certainly look smug to me as well,' Charlie stood facing him, waiting for an answer.

'I've heard Sir, they've found the girl.'

'Fantastic!' Charlie hollered without thinking. 'Is she okay?'

'Yes, fit and well; if not a little embarrassed for doing a runner.'

'Where was she?' Cliff urged.

'The Lake District. She'd absconded with the school's part time music teacher and taken off in his VW Camper and, as she described it, to see the world. They tracked them down near Selside Pike parked in a gateway. A local bobby thought it was strange when he glimpsed a young girl in school uniform crapping at the road side. She seemed happy to come home complaining that the camper van's heater had packed up and, having only her uniform, Coniston Water in November wasn't her idea of seeing the world. She said his blues guitar playing was driving her crazy.

'Jack also mentioned that Conrad from the Journal called in at the station to see you Sir. He said that while his reporter Andrew Maunder, was digging into the background of our Clarence in the regional press, he discovered an article on Clarence's wife, Grace Nancekivell. The British Newspaper Archive had a record of an article from way back in 1973 in The Somerset Gazette. It referred to The Oaks Clinic on the outskirts of Taunton, where she was admitted following a disturbance which occurred in Weston-Super-Mare. The police removed her from the sea front parade for the protection of both herself and the public at large. She was detained at the Police Station where she was examined and interviewed by a doctor and social worker, who believed she was suffering from a mental disorder, and needed to be temporarily admitted for her own safety and an assessment.' Beer paused, 'I'm pretty sure that's it, only Jack did rattle on.'

'What was she doing?' Charlie said.

'He didn't say. Only that the report stated that her husband Clarence intervened, requesting her discharge.'

'All a waste of time.' Cliff contributed, 'I've had moments when I've come close to exploding, I guess we all have, and if you tell the so-called experts what they want to hear, spinning them some sort of yarn, then they're happy.'

'Always the cynical bugger.' Charlie said.

Peace descended, either as a result of their contemplation of the news, or just plain tiredness, Beer wasn't sure.

'So having a bit of time on my hands and the use of Charlotte's computer I did a spot of research.'

'And?' Cliff said half-heartedly.

'I explored the characteristics of a sociopath and…"

'A sociopath?' Cliff interrupted.

Charlie joined in, 'Let the lad have his head.'

'Well Boss, it's someone who exhibits antisocial behaviours and attitudes. They are often impulsive, aggressive, irresponsible and have a warped capacity for love, even to their nearest. Their feelings are generally superficial and lack any empathy, seeing others as those to be controlled and manipulated along with lying for their own personal gain. They may well be convinced in their inability to make a success of their own life and typically have no sense of conscience, guilt, or remorse. They can also have a tendency towards harmful acts whilst experiencing no problem or shame.' He closed his notebook.

'But Francesca was nearly in tears when we talked about Clarence?' Charlie prompted.

'Sure, but according to the research their tears may not represent any emotional depth,' Beer said, 'rather actions they can use to their advantage.'

'In hindsight, it would be very hard to argue that Francesca didn't possess many of their traits.' Cliff had to admit adding, 'I wonder?'

'What?' Charlie said.

'Oh, just something Charlotte said back along,' and proceeded to leave it there. 'I don't know if Francesca's experiences are of her imagination, vicarious rather than the truth.'

'Do you trust her word? Do you believe her?' Charlie delved.

Cliff thought.

'I trust that she believes it or perhaps has learnt to but I still don't totally believe her and it would be wrong to take her account at face value. Maybe we've got to be thinking of what we've never before considered. If you've done something you don't like or want to believe, you overlook it, regarding it as someone else's fault. We block it out. I believe our questioning is resurrecting her hidden ghosts, her inner secrets.'

Charlie seemed almost convinced.

'According to the psychologist, Carl Jung,' Beer's words heralded his final pitch on the subject. 'The dark side of our unconscious refers to all the unacceptable and undesirable aspects of our personality.'

'You certainly had some time on your hands, didn't you?' Cliff jeered.

Charlie instantly came back, 'Don't give the lad too hard a time otherwise he'll chuck the job in.'

'You're right. You won't do that will you Beer?'

'No Boss, my skin's tougher than that.'

'Good. Only I don't know what I'd do without you,' and Cliff kind of coughed.

'We've absolutely no proof she was involved. She says she arrived after it happened and we've no evidence to the contrary. I just can't help thinking she's playing the long game.' Charlie concluded.

'She seemed totally weird over the death; it felt all wrong,' admitted Cliff. 'I'm certain a bit of the puzzle is still missing.'

'Why do you say that, Cliff?' Charlie stressed.

'I believe that her saying Clarence fell and it was an accident, isn't the truth. Why not report it? Why not tell us that in the beginning? And there was no reaction to the fact that a fatal blow to Clarence's head had killed him before he hit the water and probably the rocks. She's not telling us everything. What do you suggest?' Cliff persisted.

Charlie sighed, 'We've delivered a verbal caution to her, citing her lying, falsifying her account and obstructing our investigations. What we need to do now is to pursue a formal caution with her, ideally getting her to the station and loosen her tongue. And we need to find Steven. His account will help us break this circle.'

Cliff said, 'That's a man I am concerned for. He's diabetic, type one, needing regular injections of insulin as well as obviously food to control his condition and maintain his health, avoiding complications which can be deadly serious. Where is he and more's to the point, how is he?'

Beer spoke, 'I never realised at the time, but when we visited Stoneycroft, I could have sworn there was an insulin pen sitting on her dresser in the kitchen. Blue, like a fat biro with a dial at one end. Isn't that weird?'

The boys silently acknowledged their worst fears. Cliff shared what each of them was thinking.

'She's lost her first-born son Brian, her husband Clarence, and now according to her, her youngest son Steven is a stranger to her whom she no longer trusts. Who's left for her? Perhaps she's even lost herself.'

THIRTY EIGHT

The boys began to make their way back up to Stoneycroft yet again. The glorious morning heralded the start of a bright new day, one which they were confident would bring a conclusion to the recent drama and antics.

Days earlier, following Clarence's death, chaotic scenes had unfolded within the walls of the cottage. Steven had returned in one hell of a state, uncontrollable, wrestling with what had happened and harbouring feelings of both remorse and relief. Understanding, Francesca attempted to console him, offering to help him get away from the island to seek support and treatment. She convinced him that anyone who had suffered for years the memories of that fateful accident, and his brother's death, and was now equally haunted by the death of his father, needed help. She calmly told him that they both needed help and she'd go with him, staying close by his side and he mustn't worry or allow himself to be troubled by endless futile questions or fears.

'I'll always be with you and we'll be fine, it will turn out okay. After all your father had slipped, it was an accident, a suicide, how on earth could we have known what he would do? We both want the same thing; to forget all that's happened and above all, be at peace.' Her words were a comfort to him. 'The body which lay on the rocks was no longer your father was it? It had no breath, it was just a corpse. This is the last we'll see of this place!'

For anyone with a messed-up head it is probable that they will be susceptible to such wild and wonderful suggestions.

As the boys spotted the cottage, their conversations unsurprisingly focussed on Francesca.

'I guess once you've lied, it's easier to keep lying,' Beer pronounced attempting at what he took to be profound logic.

'The more we heard from her, the more confused she seemed,' Charlie said, certain that taking her into custody would be the smart thing to do.

Cliff still had lingering doubts about the woman.

'She doesn't entirely make sense. On one hand she would have us believe she still has feelings for her husband and her only son and yet Clarence wanted to divorce her and Steven had turned into some kind of monster. He had become a serious problem, originally for his mother, Grace, and now was turning out to be a real liability for her on the island. I can't help thinking that sooner or later something else is going to happen.'
Charlie shared what each was thinking.

'But what?'

'Charlotte said something,' Cliff remarked, almost inconsequentially. 'When Charlotte called on Francesca to see if she wanted her to sit in on our interview with her as a kind of support, she found her busy cleaning through the cottage.'

'What's unusual about that?' Beer said.

'Charlotte said she was sure Francesca had been drinking, there was a whiff of brandy on her breath, and Charlotte commented how she seemed different, with an air of superiority.'

They arrived at Stoneycroft and knocking on its side door, waited; their talk reflecting on the change in the weather. After a minute or two they knocked again and trying the door, found it bolted. By now, Beer had strolled to the front of the cottage.

'This door's locked too and doesn't look as though it opens. I'll check the windows.'

'Fine!' Cliff called and turning to Charlie said, 'That's odd, I swear I can hear a radio.'

Beer joined them, 'I've tried all the windows and none budge and I can't see a sign of anyone.'

'I'm certain she wasn't in the village when we left. I checked the store and the Tavern, and after all, it's only eight-thirty.'

'Right.' Charlie said acknowledging Cliff. 'Maybe she just wants us to go away?'

'Maybe,' Cliff said, 'although I can't believe she's got wind of us taking her off the island.'

'There's only one thing for it,' Charlie declared, 'we need to force the door, who knows, perhaps she's collapsed or had an accident,' he added as if a concern for her safety, no matter how tenuous it might in future justify their actions.

The door gave way easily and the three entered, separating to explore the cottage's five rooms.

A small Roberts portable, perched on the sill behind the kitchen sink, was broadcasting lively popular music, while an ancient washing machine gyrated and whirled attempting to compete. A neat pile of well ironed clothes lay on the Formica table with a full wicker basket of garments waiting their turn on the floor below. Two crisp white shirts on hangers were hooked on one of the adjoining room doors and as Beer opened it, one fell to the floor.

'It's a man's,' he shared with surprise.

Each one in turn called out:

'No-one here!' Charlie said.

'Nope, nor here!'

'No-one!'

Charlie was in the snug where they had chatted to Francesca the day before. Cliff entered the front bedroom to be faced with a stripped mattress and little else other than a sealed white envelope addressed to, 'Detective Cranford Cliff' and marked 'personal'. He thought it was weird that anyone would leave a message for him.

'You've got to look at this!' Beer shouted from the shower room. The room wasn't spacious but every flat surface: the floor, shower tray and shelf displayed remnants of cleaning - scrubbing brushes and scouring pads, a mop and brush, cloths of all types, an empty jug, a handful of disinfectant bottles, some clearly empty others half full, towels and cleaning liquid. All sorts of debris. They looked on confused, amazed.

'Why is the place so tidy?' Beer said.

It appeared to be the result of some kind of siege mentality they thought.

'The kettle is still warm!' Charlie declared. 'She, or someone else who was here, can't be far.'

Cliff exclaimed, 'The Lighthouse' and turning to Beer said, 'you need to get up there. Your legs are younger than ours. Get up to the top and see if you can spot her. As quick as you can lad.'

Towering some 97 feet perched on the summit of Chapel Hill, the impressive granite lighthouse commanded a stunning 360 degree panoramic view of the whole island, across the Bristol Channel and beyond. Decommissioned at the end of the 1800s, this one time, Keeper's tower now served as a 'daymark' for shipping, and a superb vantage for visitors. Beer clambered up its curling staircase, nearly 150 winding steps. The few wooden windows lit his way and offered glimpses of the island as he climbed to its lantern room and onto the open balcony. Breathless he momentarily froze, taking in the phenomenal views. He scanned the island, looking for any evidence of Francesca. After several minutes, Beer emerged back down and joined them, hot and bothered.

'I'd not been up there before and can't believe how breathtaking it was, way out to Devon and Cornwall and the Welsh coast.'

'Sure, but did you spot her?' Cliff was starting to become a spot impatient with the lad.

'No, I scanned the island but no sign of her, Boss.'

Cliff was afraid of that, yet it wasn't unexpected.

'Oh, and what did the letter say?' Beer ventured, curious to know what they'd learnt in his absence.

'I'll read it to you both if you like then you can see what you make of it.

My Friend,'

Cliff coughed and cleared his throat before he continued.

'I had loved my Steven, we were family but thinking that was as far as it went. He was unwelcome back in my life. I wanted solitude, freedom from the demons that entrapped him. What he had done had changed him and I grieve to see the way he is now; domineering and full of hatred.

I brought him to this world, to live amongst others and now I wish he had died inside me, my once loved son who I no longer know. Every time I look into his eyes, I feel sick with guilt. I could no longer face him and what he might do, not only to me, but others. One crime can so easily lead to another as we try to cover our evil ways and I couldn't be sure that was the end of it for Steven.

As for me I didn't use to be evil, but that is what I realise now he has made me. I can't live with that, I had to do something, so I decided to let it end with me. Sometimes you have to do what you think you can't, it's a responsibility, a duty out of so called love. The reality of what we had done was more than I knew I could bear or live with. When you're faced with a monster you have no alternative, you have to stop it. I couldn't save Steven from himself, but I could save him from the world. I can no longer stay on the island, not now. The peace and spirit of Lundy is lost to me forever.

As I told you Mr Detective, Steven is still here, he never left, but he will never be able to tell you what happened.

'The letter's signed, Francesca.'

Cliff reflected for a moment.

'Do you believe she wrote it, Boss?'

'Yes. I've no reason not to think that,' Cliff said, appearing disturbed.

'What is it, Boss?'

Cliff took a brief moment before he replied. 'I feel fortune has deserted me along with any faith I had in humanity, Beer.'

'The letter has a dark evil note to it that's for sure,' Charlie said.

'Can you trust what she has written, Boss?'

'Yes. I believe for the first time it's the truth, Beer. I can only imagine what she has done.'

'It's rarely one gets an insight into the mind of a murderer.' Charlie said.

Cliff handed the letter to Beer. You'd better pass it on to SOCO as evidence. I think I need to get some air.'

'Right. I guess it's hard to know what she'll do next.' Beer said with deep concern.

'It's uncanny but I can't help thinking I know where she's gone.' While the other two looked on unconvinced

Cliff started to stride out towards the steep escarpment where only a day earlier he and Charlotte had clambered over the rocky path.

'Why this way?' Charlie said following him.

'When I saw the cottage, I couldn't help thinking everything had changed with her. It felt wrong. Whatever was filling her head, call it a compulsion or maybe even a demon, had been let loose and couldn't be stopped.' Charlie didn't question Cliff's assessment but concentrated on breathing deeply, as he tried to keep up.

By now Beer, having guessed their destination, was pulling ahead of the two old men.

Cliff's pace quickened and his stride lengthened. Charlie stumbled on the uneven ground, then regained his balance. He'd only been on the go a few minutes but not being the athletic type was already feeling the strain.

'You go on Cliff, I'll catch up,' he said gasping. They could see Beer in the middle distance, his solitary figure was now nearing the edge.

Cliff called out to him, 'Further' and pointed. Beer waved back frantically.

Cliff tried to pace himself, conscious he was feeling far from well. His shirt began to feel clammy and clung to him. Turning, he saw Charlie walking. Beer called but his words were unclear. Cliff became anxious, nervous as to what the lad had seen, for some reason he sensed something awful. As he reached Beer's side he looked down and there far below a body lay, spread upon the rocks. If they had only acted sooner, maybe this wouldn't have happened. The two stood speechless.

'Suicide?' Charlie said drawing beside them.

'Although we can't rule out an accident, perhaps a fall.' Cliff said with more than a degree of regret in his voice.

Beer appealed, 'We don't know where Steven is and if he was involved, isn't that right?'

'Yes, that's right,' Cliff confessed.

'When you started out Boss, was this what you expected to find?'

'No, not what I expected, but if I'm honest what I dreaded. It seems weirdly significant that Francesca has gone the same way as her husband, Clarence.'

'Maybe there's a kind of justice in that,' Charlie surmised, 'and even now we still have nothing to incriminate her in his death. This case was never perfectly straightforward and with what's happened, it's become even more complicated.'

A taste of salt hung heavy in the air that greeted them as they gazed down, but in no time a breeze had stiffened and refreshed the winter's day.

THIRTY NINE

'I think we're done here.' Charlie said. 'Beer, get back to the cottage and grab the binoculars I saw in her snug. We need to be sure she's well and truly dead, then I'll call this one in.'

While they waited for Beer the two speculated.

Cliff spoke first, 'I couldn't help thinking she wasn't lying about Steven being near, here on the island.'

'What makes you say that?' Charlie said, somewhat doubtful.

'Didn't you notice? She did a little thing at times when I think she was lying.'

'What thing?' Charlie said, questioning both his own and Cliff's powers of observation.

'You sound as if you think I'm delusional?'

'No, not really. I am just sceptical.'

'With her fingers, I'm sure she appeared to rub them together against her thumb. I admit it was hardly noticeable. Anyway, that's what I reckon.' Cliff looked at Charlie expectantly.

'It was unnoticeable to me,' Charlie admitted still unsure.

Francesca's comment regarding Steven still played heavily on Cliff's mind. 'Why tell us Steven was here if he wasn't?'

'To mislead us.'

'Why say anything?' Charlie looked baffled and shrugged.

'Well, I believe he is still here, on the island somewhere,' Cliff went on, trying to explain his reasoning. 'That's the rational answer. How would he have got off?' No-one's left on the ship that we don't know about and you can't board the boat without a boarding pass which you need a ticket for. No other boats have landed since we discovered the body, and there hasn't been a helicopter flight that we haven't known about or the I.D. of any of the passengers.'

'Okay, so what now?' Charlie said equally bemused.

'We find him and end this whole thing.'

Beer returned breathing heavily. He focussed the binoculars, gazed down and pronounced, 'No signs of her being alive Sir and there's a lot of blood on the rocks around her head.' Beer seemed to fuss with the glasses. 'Shit. It's a man!'

Cliff grabbed the glasses.

'Shit, you're right. We need to get someone down there to check if he's still alive. Where the body is, it doesn't look as if he'll be washed off by the waves, but it's critical we drape some sacking over the body, or a tarp, to keep those pesky gulls off.' The gulls were now exercising excitedly overhead, executing some impressive barrel rolls in anticipation.

Charlie exclaimed, 'Bugger me! I'll get hold of SOCO in Barnstaple, we need them over now.'

He was already rehearsing in his head how best to release the news to the press.

Cliff said, 'I'll ask Charlotte and see if she can organise someone to go down to him. Beer, you get back to the cottage and secure it until the crime scene boys get here. I don't want anyone in there noseying around.'

'Charlotte, we've discovered another body lying on the rocks near Pilot's Quay.' Cliff gave her no time to respond. 'We need to check if they're alive and cover it over until forensic get here. Eventually we'll have to recover the body. In the meantime, it seems pretty likely Francesca is still on the island. We don't think she's going to be able to return to the cottage so have you any ideas where she might hold out? Where do we look?'

Mindful that Francesca would not want to be found a shocked Charlotte identified the most likely locations. After a couple of radio calls the arrangements had been made.

'So, where are we Cliff?' With the three coppers having congregated in the office, Charlie was wanting to get to grips with the plan.

'Charlotte's organised the Island's Fire and Rescue crew to fix up ropes at the scene and to go down to the body; they are on their way there in the Land Rover as we speak. Jago's taking a quad and checking Tibbetts, the old

Admiralty Station up the north end, the Gun Battery on the west coast, and Benson's Cave. Charlotte's going to check out the disused Timekeeper's Hut near the quarry on the east side, as well as the derelict Old Hospital remains while Beer, you can re-check the church, maybe have a chat to Bridget there to see if she's seen anything.'

'If you like Cliff, I can oversee the rope crew,' Charlie volunteered. 'Will Charlotte be alright on her own only we don't know what Francesca's capable of?'

'Sure, good point, I'll go with Charlotte,' Cliff said, 'let's rendezvous here, say 6.00pm?'

Two hours later, with a squeal of brakes and screech of tyres, the quad returned with Jago looking agitated.

'Not a sign!' he shared with Cliff and Charlotte. 'And you guys?'

'Nothing!' they said.

'There's just Beer, but I don't hold out much hope there,' Cliff admitted.

Moments later Beer joined them reporting, 'no joy.'

Charlie arrived shortly after.

'Guess what?' It was abundantly clear none of the others had any idea. 'I called through to Barnstaple and…' Charlie waited before dropping the bombshell, 'The Crime Scene bods already knew about the death, someone had called it in to Bideford.'

'When did that happen?' Cliff said, the amazement clearly evident in his voice.

'This morning at 8.00am.' Charlie admitted equally amazed.

'That's strange, but we didn't find the body until mid morning.'

'The caller didn't say who had been killed, just that it was on Lundy.'

'Who was it that called?'

'No name.'

'A man or a woman's voice?'

'They thought at the Nick that it was a woman.'

'Hell fire!' Cliff exclaimed.

Charlotte interrupted proceedings, 'While we were out hunting around the island someone must have slipped this note into the office. I've only just discovered it; it's addressed to you Cliff.'

Cliff perused the envelope and as he tore it open and glimpsed the contents, he was speechless.

'Not another letter. What does this one say Cliff?' Charlie insisted, trying to get a word out of him.

'I didn't see that coming,' Cliff said as he began to read. Looking alarmed, he turned to Charlie and Beer. 'They say they have no intention of giving themselves up and he hasn't finished his killing.'

'Who?' Charlie barked with a volume that could have been heard in the adjoining Tavern.

'No name,' Cliff disclosed.

Beer's heart sank, 'Do you believe them?'

'I don't know. The grammar and punctuation are hardly great, nor the handwriting, but it's too risky not to,' Cliff said. 'They want to talk to me and the papers as well as TV.'

'What a bloody awful mess,' Charlie blurted.

FORTY

The islanders of Lundy had been shocked by the first murder. Everyone seemed to think it would be solved in no time. Now there was another death much like the first, and this was bound to shake the very foundation of the island's community.

'It won't be long before everyone knows. Something must be said before rumours start circulating,' Charlotte implored, 'and there needs to be a renewed confidence in the police and sense of security.'

Her plea wasn't ignored. Charlie and Cliff immediately considered the possibility of a meeting with all on the island, to allay any fears.

'Fear is a funny old thing,' Beer said. 'It's what your brain tells you, that's where the fear is.'

The other two thought Beer's familiarity with the finer workings of the brain was hard to comprehend.

They logically concluded the best place for such a meeting was St Helens. It was large enough and restricting attendance to the islanders would avoid the odd inquisitive visitor who might well prove to be a complication, perhaps even a disruption. The gathering would provide the opportunity for folk to ask questions and for the police to assure everyone they were on top of the case even though the reality was they weren't! They could also appeal for help in finding Francesca.

'After all,' Charlie said, 'the vast majority of murderers are known to not only their victims, but also to their neighbours and friends.'

'I suppose that makes perfect sense.' Charlotte said while sipping her coffee.

'I still can't quite fathom why he would jump off a cliff and kill himself,' Beer shared almost as an afterthought.

'It will only be the evidence that will prove if he did, or whether perhaps there was a fight and he was pushed. To know that, we wait on the doc's wise words,' Cliff admitted.

'How did your flight over go this time, Doc? Quite a buzz I'd guess?' Cliff trod carefully unsure of the old boy's reaction.

'I'm trying to get over it. The previous pilot seemed positively sane compared to this chap. I'm sure they are well used to the flight but the only buzz I got was a string of worrying concerns in my head about aircraft safety and inadequate maintenance, the pilot's expertise, the impending weather, air accident figures and how long it would take for the lifeboat to reach us from Appledore. I can tell you it certainly isn't any longer on my bucket list!'

'But surely you felt safe?' Cliff enquired with a degree of mischief trying to retrieve the situation.

'Oh the pilot said, 'It's not dangerous,' as he revved the engine prior to take-off but he couldn't leave it there. He had to add, 'Well, it's not dangerous unless you consider an airplane flight or car ride or walking out of your front door as dangerous.' And then crowned it by adding, 'Safety is our paramount concern!' As we took to the air he went on to explain, 'It is considerably more dangerous than airline travel but far safer than riding in a car,' and as if I could decide exactly how dangerous it really was said, 'Mind you helicopters are much harder to fly than an aircraft; it's a bit like trying to balance on a floating beach ball.' The guy's a menace not only to the tourism industry but to mankind at large!'

Within the hour the doc had downed two mugs of well sugared strong black coffee along with six digestives and, intent on returning to the mainland on the boat bringing out the SOCO boys in a couple of hours, was soon standing at the cliff top waiting to be briefed. He knew full well that the forensic opportunities were at their best as soon as possible after death.

'To where we start our roped decent, there's a short pitch down over rough terrain,' the Rescue Leader explained, 'it's a bit awkward and a scramble but dry under foot and I don't think you'll find it too tough. Are you okay with that?'

'Sure,' doc said lacking total conviction and in two minds as to whether his trip was a mistake.

'Great! It's a low tide and the swell is only a couple of feet. We've set up a rope anchor station, a sling around a rock at the top of the drop and from there you'll abseil down the cliff. It's steep but you'll be roped on and perfectly safe.'

For a nervous moment doc thought - there they go again with this 'safe' thing.

The leader continued. 'You'll be lowered in a controlled descent of about 340 feet,' he could see the doc was looking increasingly uneasy so decided to inject some fun into the proceedings.

'If it all goes pear-shaped, you'll end up in the water. You can swim can't you, that is assuming you're still able?'

The doc was silent.

'When you get down to the rocks, I'll be there to steady you. Although the swell is low, we need to watch the waves as we'll be exposed. Let's carry out a final check that the helmet is snug and firmly fastened, your harness is tight and not kinked or buckled, carabiners are locked, your belay device is correctly orientated and the rope isn't twisted. It's tough and won't stretch and all the knots are good. What about your shoes? It would be best if you wear something more appropriate; here, try these running shoes, there's a couple of sizes. Use your feet and try to look for the best foot holds and keep your back straight and reasonably upright to the rock face, well as near as you can, and shoulders back. As you descend, use your feet on the cliff face to steady yourself and reduce any swing. Okay?'

The doc, a natural procrastinator, looked hesitant and pale.

'I wouldn't say we're experts but we've done this loads of times before. We'll bring you up the same way as you go down.'

Had the doc previously been in any doubt as to whether this was a good idea, he was quite certain now that it wasn't.

'What did you discover Doc?' Cliff and Charlie were understandably keen to know.

'I haven't got the psyche for all these dangerous adventures,' and with that he cupped his hands, lit a cigarette, took a dep drag and puffed as a spiralling whiff of smoke drifted skyward.

'I didn't think you smoked?'

'I don't,' doc said burning his fingers on the match.

The doc then began explaining his preliminary findings:

'He exhibits a number of contusions, some severe, not unexpected considering the fall and impact encountered. Regarding the colouring of his bruises, some are definitely older, maybe in the past week or more, those on the underside of his arms and the back of the legs. Of course he might well bruise very easily however, the position at the older bruises suggests that they are as a result of some kind of physical trauma. I can't categorically state that the other bruising occurred before or after death and can't at this stage see any evidence of foul play although it must not be ruled out. There aren't any contusions about the neck which would suggest strangulation. In summary my initial findings suggest he died as a result of the fall cracking open his head, it's funny how that can be fatal.'

'You say funny Doc,' Cliff said, 'but you don't mean funny ha ha do you?'

'Certainly not. When I get the body back to the lab I will be able to tell you more. Undoubtedly, he will have significant internal injuries after such a fall and I'll be able to come up with an approximate time of death.'

'I think we probably know that Doc.' Cliff said reticently, 'I would say that he died between around eight and ten thirty.'

'The rescue team anticipate bringing up the body after SOCO have done their stuff; they're on their way heading out on a fast charter boat and will be here in the hour. They'll search the cliff top and the cottage and any evidence retrieved goes back to the forensic boys,' Charlie confirmed.

Almost incidentally as an after-thought, the doc piped up,

'And that's how I should have got here, on a fast boat,' the regret was clearly evident in his voice.

In no time two of the SOCO team had reached the cliff top where one began scouring for any shred of evidence while the second abseiled down to search the rocks where the body lay. Equipped with a rubberised body bag, the officer and climber finally bagged the corpse, overseeing it being hauled back up the cliff.

The other two SOCO members headed for the cottage around which they systematically draped yellow 'Crime Scene' police tape. As it fluttered in the light breeze, it weirdly looked like some funfair attraction. Beer was taken aback to see all their paraphernalia – tools, cameras, lights and metal cases full of, he didn't know what. As they changed into their white overalls, images of TV detective shows came to mind. He had never witnessed anything like this before in his brief crime fighting career.

FORTY ONE

To the rear of Stoneycroft was a small timber clad shed with a corroded corrugated pent roof. As the officers entered, they were immediately struck by an obnoxious stink, one that neither could place. Before them were displayed the usual array of well used garden tools, propped on the boarded floor as if sentries awaiting their orders. All manner of odds and sods packed the numerous shelves, bowing under their own weight. What was particularly odd was finding an old pack of Rodenticide because there were no rats on Lundy. The only other occupants crammed into the tiny shed was a tired looking push lawn mower, proudly boasting an aged patina and a compact chest freezer. Its cabinet had given way to a growing invasion of browning rust, flaking its one time white gloss finish. Much to their surprise a thick mysterious brown red fluid appeared to have been seeping from beneath the cabinet. Its presence probably accounting for the strong smell. The glutinous consistency of the solution suggested that it had been leaking for some time. The cabinet's lid was fitted with a hasp and staple, united with an antique Yale padlock. As one of the men attempted to persuade the padlock's shackle to give way, another shared their ideas as to what could be causing the discharge in the chest.

'I've seen something like this before. It was gross!'

'What was it, what did you see?'

'Blood. Watered down blood,' he declared.

His colleague, who had been trying to cut through the lock plate faltered in his endeavours on hearing the word 'blood!'

'And?' he said.

'It was at home. Whilst we were away for a weekend unbeknown to us there had been a power cut. Consequently, the joints of meat my wife had stored in our freezer had completely defrosted. The bottom of our chest freezer was pooled with bloody water which had started to seep out of the drainage outlet. But it wasn't as bad as this.'

His colleague put him straight. 'But the freezer is on.'

'Yes, but didn't you know folks here don't have any electricity supply late at night until dawn. If the freezer is not full and whatever's in there is only partly frozen, it could easily defrost in a cabinet this size in, say six to seven hours, and after all it's not that cold in here, is it? Fluctuations in temperature like that can lead to a slow decomposition of the flesh.'

'I think before we do anything else we ought to dust the lid and look for prints.'

'Good idea, that's a lot of fluid.'

'If there was something alive in there how long would it survive?'

'First there would be a constriction of the blood vessels due to the low temperature causing a lack of the necessary blood circulation. Next, excruciating pain as the heart, lungs and brain ceased functioning. But sooner than that they would have trouble breathing. The lid's been designed to be airtight. As your body gets cold you will use more oxygen and therefore, there would quickly be a build-up of carbon dioxide.'

They both stopped what they were doing and again studied the puddle which seemed even more menacing.

'What do you think?'

'It's hard to believe, although they did say there was someone involved in the case missing on the island.'

At the first opportunity of meeting up with Charlie, Cliff asked him, 'Any ID on the body stranded on the rocks?'

'No name.'

'I suppose it's a fair bet it is Steven,' Cliff said.

'I've asked the doc to send the best shots of the face to Jack so he can get the Carmarthenshire lot to check it out. It's a bit of a mess but enough to get a likeness. What about you?'

'I've been trying to fathom the cryptic message from the so-called killer and now I'm told Marion's desperate to talk to me.'

'Marion?' Charlie had difficulty in placing the woman.

'She's in the kitchen, allegedly one of Francesca's so-called mates.'

'What does she want to talk about? Charlie persisted.

'Absolutely no idea.'

'Right, well let's find out.'

A few minutes later they were joined by Marion.

'This is Charlie Harris, Marion, my Sarge. I doubt you've met.'

'I'm just Charlie.'

Marion, with a bemused look, shook his hand.

'So why the urgency, you've got us all guessing.' Cliff admitted. Marion remained silent.

'Are you okay with me here Marion?' Charlie said, 'and be assured what you tell us remains within these walls.'

Marion wasn't looking for the reassurance, she expected it and relaxed somewhat on hearing Charlie's words.

'It's about the note.'

'Note?' Cliff attempted trying to clarify precisely what she had in mind before they jumped to conclusions.

'The note from the killer,' she bleated.

'What note is that?' Charlie offered trying to appear vague, bewildered.

'So, that's it, is it, we're playing games, are we?'

Cliff caught Charlie's gaze and attempted to ease the atmosphere.

'I'm sorry you feel like that, it's not our intention and please appreciate that if you know anything, anything at all, we need to know.'

'I know who wrote it,' she shared with a degree of satisfaction.

Charlie whimpered under his breath, just enough for Marion to notice.

'That's shaken you, hasn't it?'

'Yes,' Cliff admitted, 'just as the note did.'

Marion came straight back, 'Well, you don't need it to.'

'Don't need to what?' Charlie joined in.

'Worry about the note.'

'Are you telling us it was a hoax, you made it up?'

'No, I didn't write it but I know the man that did write it.'

'Where's that Beer when you need him?' Cliff's frustration was evident. 'We need to find Marion's guy Charlie and question him and put a stop to his madness before he does something else stupid.'

'Just leave it to me,' Charlie volunteered, 'I'll grab Charlotte and track him down. You stay to field any other developments, that's if there could possibly be anymore!'

Cliff was unable to settle, pacing back and forth in the office turning over countless scenarios and getting nowhere. After what seemed an endless fifteen minutes he slumped in a chair, mentally exhausted. Cliff was totally unaware of how the numerous faces and places which occupied his mind were playing havoc with his subconscious.

'Okay Boss?' Beer's timely words broke Cliff's oppressive mood.

'Have you been up at the cottage all this time?'

'Yes. The officers wanted me on hand in case something significant turned up.'

'And did it?'

'Maybe. They discovered a load of documents, including what looks like a driving licence that had been burnt in the wood burner, and I left them trying to crack open a locked chest freezer cabinet in the shed which they have a bad feeling about.

FORTY TWO

One of the Scenes of Crimes Officer's tenacity, ingenuity and disparate endeavours had finally paid-off; the freezer's lid was free, free to be opened. He had been so engrossed in the task that little consideration had been given to what might be revealed.

He rubbed his eyes, closed them, then focussed on the lid. For a man who was well used to managing surprises he feared that there might be more than enough awaiting him in the cabinet. For some reason the uncertainty in this instance was proving almost too much, after all there had already been two deaths on this tiny island. But it was more than that, how grim would his discovery be? His heart started to speed-up. He threw open the lid to reveal large hunks of bloodied flesh, randomly sprawled across the freezer's bottom. They lay submerged in pools of semi-congealed blood.

The smell was overwhelming, he wretched and stepped back. Spontaneously his colleague swung open the shed door and a fresh breeze poured in refreshing the atmosphere and filled their lungs as the men steadied themselves, coming to terms with the gory remains before then. Had it not been for the labelling on the bagged joints, they would have instantly thought the worst.

'That certainly looks like lamb to me!' one shared with the other, relieved.

Once again, the middled-aged, heavy weight Roy appeared before Cliff and Beer but this time Charlie joined in on what would prove to be a memorable interview. Roy moved uneasily, fidgeting uncomfortably on a stool which Cliff had deliberately chosen for him.

'So Roy, it's a crying shame we had to drag you in for a chat again only I'm sure you will appreciate it's not every day we get a note from a murderer.'

As Roy scanned the three, it was impossible not to grasp the seriousness of the occasion; the sergeant's stern expression further confirmed that for him.

Roy blustered, 'I don't know what...' but Cliff was having none of it and interrupted.

'You won't be surprised to see this Roy,' thrusting the threatening note before him. 'This is from you, isn't it? How can you live haunted by the ghostly dead bodies on your conscience?'

Wiping the beads of perspiration from his face with what looked like his usual oily handkerchief, Roy wheezed and managed,

'I've never seen this before.'

'Really, is that so?' Cliff countered, 'yet your body language, along with our witness tells us to the contrary as I suspect will finger print analysis.'

By now Charlie had also had enough.

'You appreciate I am sure, that this is very serious. It's not only about wasting police time and disrupting our investigations, but I am increasingly inclined to believe you are the murderer.'

Roy's face turned white. He glared and noticeably recoiled on the stool, nearly falling off. This tubby guy's prank had well and truly backfired and somehow, he was unable to see a way out without appearing the fool he in all honestly was. Cliff appreciated this and threw him a life-line.

'What made you do it Roy, is it because you wanted to be important?'

Roy grimaced and snapped, 'Yes! I'm the resident engineer, just one of them, no one takes me seriously or sees me as...' his explanation tailed away.

'So, we take it Roy that you wrote it, and you've not murdered anyone or intend to kill anyone, is that right?'

An embarrassed Roy nodded.

'For the record you need to answer Roy.'

'Yes, I never have or intend to kill anyone.'

He waited to be told the consequences of his actions and the three of them decided it would do him good to wait.

'The doc's telephone call explained that his preliminary examinations of the dead man suggested a substance may be present in his body.' Cliff went on to expand on the doc's findings. 'The dosage whilst not toxic enough to cause death indicates the level was sufficient to result in visible changes in the skin; darkening of the flesh and lesions, especially on the hands, and thickening of the skin. Typically, this might be as a result of arsenic poisoning. Early blood tests support this hypothesis but they need to undertake further tests, including urine, which will take a few more days. Other side effects of this might include increased anxiety, cognitive impairment, abdominal pain, nausea; vomiting, diarrhoea, severe fluid loss, and longer term more seriously, heart problems and cancer.

'I asked him what could be the likely source of the toxin arsenic. He concluded it could be rat bait, qualifying his assumption that the SOCO team recorded the presence of Rodenticide, which contains arsenic, in Francesca's shed. I presumed it wasn't likely to happen accidently and the doc agreed it was most unlikely, although it couldn't categorically be ruled out.'

'So why feed it to Steven?' Beer said.

'It seems that it would result in weakening him both physically and mentally,' Cliff clarified.

At that moment the office fax machine sprung into life, beeping and screeching as it churned out its message. Beer lifted the page and started to read.

'Jack's just sent this to you Sir,' and he handed it to Charlie. Charlie perused its contents.

'Basically, the head and face of the body were both so badly mutilated and the face contorted that I got SOCO to photograph the corpse from every angle as well as close up.' Charlie explained. 'It seems the likeness was good enough for the Llandovery lads to get a positive ID from both Steven Coles' neighbours and his mate, Huw Jones. It's rather spooky but it seems the only thing found on the body, in his trouser pocket was a diabetic's Nova insulin lancet pen.'

Charlie looked towards Cliff and Beer expectantly, 'I've been in the Force for thirty three years now man and boy, and I've never seen anything like what I saw that day on the rocks.' He considered, 'Apart from a couple of RTAs, the only other dead body was a chap who had fallen off a beach hut roof when fixing a TV aerial. He broke his neck. Nasty job and a massive shock to his missus who was in the hut trying to tune the telly.'

FORTY THREE

'I've given some thought to the island meeting in St Helen's. Have a look at the draft programme Charlie, see what you think? It's vital we do our best to dispel any fears, addressing islanders concerns in light of the two recent deaths.'

'Too many deaths, too many murders,' Charlie exclaimed to Cliff.

'Yes, but it's important we down-play that as much as possible. By sharing updates on our investigations, we can take the opportunity to address their concerns and any rumours as well as advising them of what we are doing and why. We also need to demonstrate we are committed to their safety and preserving the ethos of the island as well as field their questions. Are you okay with that, Charlie?'

'Sure,' Charlie said, 'How much should we share about the victims and suspects do you reckon?'

'We can tell them we have a crucial lead which we are pursuing, and are currently gathering vital evidence but are unable at this time to share all the details of our investigations. We can assure them we are endeavouring to be as transparent and open as far as possible with our communications, and will regularly update Peter Robinson, Charlotte Thomas and the Reverend Cleave on future developments. What do you think Charlie, glance over it?'

Before Charlie had a chance to respond Charlotte entered, disturbing their concentration.

'There's been an urgent message from the Shore Office, they called relaying a transmission from the Oldenburgh; they've a surprise visitor on board!'

Cliff and Charlie reeled at Charlotte's news.

'Who?' Cliff said.

'They wouldn't say but wanted the police to contact them urgently.'

'Are they still at the quay?'

'No, they sailed forty minutes back and are steaming for Bideford.'

'How can I talk with them?' Cliff asked.

'If I telephone the Shore Office, they can kind of patch you through on the Ship-to-Shore VHF to the Captain.' Charlotte explained.

Cliff's call lasted some ten minutes and after, he briefed Charlie of the latest.

'When the steward checked the tickets, he discovered an anomaly. He hadn't noticed one of the return tickets had long since expired. Previously he would only do this back at the Quay Office but with the restrictions on travel he now checked them en route. With only 24 on board, hardly a tenth of the ship's normal passenger capacity, it proved easy to compare the actual passengers to the agreed manifest. He soon realised there was one who neither had a valid ticket or was listed. Guess who… Francesca. At this point in time, they haven't said anything to her and I've told them to leave it that way. I can tell you she's not going to escape me that easily this time, Charlie.'

'They need to come back.'

'It's not that straight forward. By the time the ship heads back here, moors up, we arrest her, then they make for Bideford again, the Captain says the timing won't be good for crossing The Bar.'

'What's the problem with The Bar?' a confused Charlie queried.

'The Captain was very clear about that. The ridge of coarse sand and gravel which runs between Northam and Braunton Burrows across the mouth of the Taw Torridge estuary, must be crossed nearing high water. Although the ship's draft is only 1.65 metres, the depth range over The Bar currently runs from 1 metre at low water and up to 7 or so at high water. If they return to Lundy, they won't reach Bideford until nearly three hours after high water on an ebbing tide. That might well be okay but with the stormy conditions and strong winds forecast later they need to press on.'

'So, what are our options Cliff?'

'The Oldenburgh is currently making just under 12 knots, the Captain could safely drop the speed, it would still be okay for The Bar and the passengers wouldn't notice any change. If we took the fast motor cruiser

SOCO came on, we could chase after them and rendezvous with the ship about 12 to 13 miles out. I've spoken on the radio with the skipper of the cruiser who's confident it is doable. What do you think?'

'What then Cliff?'

'I'd arrest her, stay on board to Bideford and get a patrol car to meet us. We should be in around 5.30pm then drive onto Barnstaple. Meanwhile the cruiser would head back to shelter off Lundy. Beer will, I am sure, be keen to come along and further develop his sea legs.'

Within 15 minutes Cliff and Beer, equipped with life jackets were departing the safe waters of Lundy's Landing Bay onboard the motor cruiser 'Odyssey', making way on the rising tide to rendezvous with the Oldenburgh.

'I have no intention of compromising my exemplary career or my highly respected reputation, that is should I ever have had either, over this protracted unsolved case.' Cliff told an anxious Beer as they headed out to sea.

The Bristol Channel is renowned for holding many surprises but fortunately none for them that day. The six berth 40 foot Trader was a bit long in the tooth having spent its twelve year life sailing Britain's west coast as far north as the Hebrides. Yet never before had the skipper or his crew undertaken such a momentous mission, which if successful, was about to change one woman's life forever. The twin Volvo Penta engines relentlessly thrust the craft onward, making way at 16 knots towards the ferry which had now reduced speed to some 9 knots. For just over the hour Beer stayed up on the aft deck, taking the air and sea spray, making every effort not to fall or be sick on what was a roller coaster of a ride. Cliff meanwhile, relaxed in the craft's comfortable, cream upholstered classic saloon with mugs of tea, diesel fumes, the lingering smell of an earlier fish lunch as well as bouts of idle chat with the skipper while considering the best way to handle Francesca.

As the Trader held off at a safe distance from the Oldenburgh, the two officers made to board the ferry much to the surprise of the few passengers on deck. The boys had been told that this was potentially a challenging and risky business, especially for Beer, from an unstable inflatable dingy. The height difference of the two vessels, as well as the swell and wind, could all add to the difficulty. One passenger had been completely unaware anything was afoot and was content she was making her escape. This illusion of hers was soon to be dashed.

Confronting the woman Cliff declared, 'I arrest you, Grace Francesca Nancekivell, on suspicion of the murder of your oldest son, Steven Coles of Llandovery, Wales, who was found dead on rocks off Lundy Island. And we wish to further question you under formal caution regarding the death of your estranged husband, Clarence Nancekivell, found approximately two weeks earlier on rocks also off Lundy Island in similar circumstances. You do not have to say anything, but it may harm your defence if you do not mention when questioned, something which you later rely on in Court. Anything you do say may be given in evidence.'

Cliff then proceeded to inform Francesca of her right to free legal advice.

She stood before them both, speechless for a moment, greatly disappointed, but in many ways not totally surprised. Cliff had decided he would eliminate any possibility of a scene publicly knowing this episode could so easily end badly.

'I'd advise you Francesca, I can be a mean sod at times and this is one of those times, so don't push me.'

There was no sign of distress or anger in her voice, 'I knew what you'd think. You thought I had jumped, didn't you?'

She waited for his reply. It was slow in coming.

'That's what I thought at first,' Cliff said, 'but the more I considered things, the more I doubted it.'

'Considered what?'

'Your character. You're self-reliant, a survivor who doesn't give up, a manipulator, a deceiver as well as being gutsy and a fighter.'

'Well, that's a fair old list to live up to,' she boasted.

Cliff eyed her, 'And now you're probably going to prison. You told me that I would never see you again and I wasn't sure I would, yet here we are!'

'So, you think of me as a murderer?' she challenged.

'It's a bit late for that now with respect, it's not what I think, it's what a jury thinks and believes, that's what will decide your future Francesca. Do you have any weapons on you?' Cliff waited.

'No,' she said.

Beer cuffed her hands behind her back and carefully checked her jacket pockets. Cliff and Beer sat either side of her for the remainder of the uneventful sailing back to Bideford Quay.

FORTY FOUR

The Custody Sargeant at Barnstaple Police Station held her gaze through the glass screen of the front desk.

'Tell me, what have we here? What's your name luv?'

Rarely would she respond to such a common endearment, but she managed, 'Francesca Nancekivell.' The Sarge began to complete the paperwork when he was interrupted.

'It's Grace Francesca Nancekivell, Sarge!'

Jim looked up, 'Right you are Cliff, tell me Nancekivell, to what do we owe this pleasure?'

'She's a murder suspect to be held in custody awaiting questioning.'

'Is she, be damned?' Jim said still scribbling down the details.

'The murder of her son and awaiting further investigations regarding the death of her husband,' Cliff enlightened.

'A possible double-murder; sounds like one of our Agatha's infamous plots.' Jim went on, 'WPC Ellis will search you before you're taken down to the custody cell. You are entitled to free legal advice and I need you to tell me if you want to take advantage of that advice and representation?'

After she had left Cliff shared with Jim, 'There's a tremendous confusion as to just how much she was involved. A confusion she herself created and played out. The greatest obstacle we have is her refusal to admit what she has done. I'm certain guilt flows freely throughout her veins, we just need her to admit it.'

Charlie phoned through to Barnstaple Police Station and eventually got hold of Cliff.

'How did it all go? I heard you boarded okay.'

'About as good as it could have done. Francesca didn't put up a fight, there would have been no point anyway. She's sitting in her cell probably thinking over what she's going to say. So far, if you pushed me, I'd say she's going to plead guilty, but who knows.'

'For both?'

'Don't know. Maybe some secrets are intended to stay secrets.'

'Wait and see what her legal comes up with.' Charlie speculated. 'Perhaps bona fide medical circumstances, lawful self-defence, maybe totally innocent of murder with suicide on both counts or just one, and Steven his father's killer with little or no evidence and no one to plead to the contrary.'

'I guess we'll see. I'm interviewing her tomorrow morning Charlie, and am determined not to let her deceive me again. By the way how did the meeting go?' Cliff delved, 'did you get bombarded with loads of difficult questions?'

'No, not at all. I think it went well even though I'd say it myself. Folk seemed at ease, although there was plenty of chatter and speculation buzzing around with mention of the second death. Your message regarding having made an arrest off the island certainly seemed to calm things down and quell any fears; so much so the deaths didn't seem to dominate the proceedings as I expected. Along with islanders revealing odd fragments of irrelevant gossip, a couple of others wanted to say something.'

'Who were they?' Cliff replied.

'Firstly, the vicar proposed that what was needed was God's Holy Spirit to be poured onto the world's troubled waters. He went on to explain that there's a wind behind each of us that takes us through life, and our wind is the power of Jesus. Well, something along those lines. Peter Robinson was there and he wanted to say a few words too, I got a transcript from him of what he said. I'll read it to you,' Charlie said.

'*Everyone here has their own idea of Lundy. Living on an island, changes ones' perspective of life. In some ways life is simpler being closer to nature, and when that happens our real selves emerge. Many visitors say that it is a different world here on Lundy, but as we have seen we are not immune to the ways of the outside world. One thing that makes us different is, as a community, we have synergy. We live our lives and work together for the benefit and strength of each other, and that's exactly what will get us through this difficult time, together.*

Then there was also this chap, a chap I had never seen before; tall, thin, weathered looking, sixties,' Charlie referred to his notes, 'one Nigel Routh. He came up to me at the end, saying he'd spoken before to both you and Beer, and asked if you were around. I told him you were tied up. He then explained that he'd told you he spent odd evenings and hours in the day up in the Old Light's Lantern Room meditating and watching the weather.'

Cliff nodded in acknowledgement, although Charlie couldn't see him.

'Recently, he thought maybe the last day or two, he had found rubbish up there; empty food packets, a water bottle and a shabby tartan blanket. It seemed odd because he didn't think, other than tourists, anyone went up there much, certainly not to sleep over. Anyway, that was it.'

'That's interesting,' Cliff said, 'I think I know who the Old Light's mystery guest was, someone who had hardly left their home but didn't want to be found.'

As Cliff entered the interview room with Beer, WPC Ellis acknowledged them both. She was quite a bit shorter than Beer, older too, dressed in a dark blue uniform with black stockings which Beer couldn't take his eyes off! Cliff however, had never seen Francesca cry before, Francesca looked up.

'Everyone I loved is dead.' Any self-defiance appeared to have melted away.

Beer switched on the tape machine and Cliff commenced the interview announcing those present.

'I see you have no legal counsel present. You are entitled to representation; can you confirm it's your choice not to be represented?'

So, the interview got underway with Francesca saying very little but admitting enough to condemn herself of involvement in the deaths at the very least.

As Beer and Cliff relaxed in the office afterwards with a cuppa, they reflected on how their time with Francesca had gone.

'Maybe she's not well,' Beer speculated, 'she seemed lost.'

'I agree.' Cliff said. 'Perhaps she believes her motives are misunderstood or that no one really cares what she thinks.' Cliff sighed deeply. 'I severely doubt that she has considered the consequence of being incarcerated for life.'

FORTY FIVE

Following more interviews with Francesca which produced little of any significance, the consensus was that she might well be the only one who would ever know what actually happened on the island. Francesca was remanded into custody at Her Majesty's Pleasure in HMP Eastwood Park in South Gloucestershire, north of Bristol. There she would stay awaiting trial. It took no time for her to realise that her new home was a world apart, exiled now from the carefree existence she enjoyed on Lundy. Here Francesca would be more alone than ever and the only way she could imagine enduring the experience was to retreat further into her own world; a world free of the crime, violence and abuse that surrounded her there.

With their business complete, Cliff and Beer hitched a ride to connect with the Hartland helicopter. The driver of the police car had a serious problem controlling his conversation. He rabbited on about anything and everything, much to the frustration of Cliff. The young constable's irritating habit had little impact on Beer who, having stretched out across the back seats, instantly drifted into a deep sleep. Beer was more than familiar with the scenic delights of the Atlantic Highway and felt it was pointless to stay awake to view them yet again. Cliff meanwhile, had to suffer a comprehensive account of the Ford Focus police car's characteristics; including its impressive acceleration, responsiveness handling and road holding and the masterful performance of the suspension and gearbox. The copper even appeared to demonstrate the vehicle's qualities by steering through some of Devon's more outrageous potholes: Beer slept through it all. As far as the officer was concerned it was a winner and he could think of nothing better than driving it all day long, although he did admit that it would be better still if there was someone to talk to.

The car gradually climbed out of town leaving the river Taw and Barnstaple behind, journeying on towards Bideford. At Bideford they took the town's new bridge, crossing the river Torridge they pressed onward inland to Higher Clovelly leaving Northam, Appledore, Westward Ho! and Buck's Mills all happily residing on Devon's North Coast. The final part of their journey once again demonstrated the attributes of the Ford as they manoeuvred the winding narrow lanes to Hartland's rocky Point. Beer woke in time to hear the constable's explanation of the pending staff changes being implemented at Barnstaple Police Station, and a concise commentary on the common sense behind it or indeed lack of sense.

Relieved, within fifteen minutes the two boys were boarding the chopper en route for the island. There below to greet them stood the solitary figure they instantly recognised as Charlotte. There was a quick wave skyward just prior to their smooth landing. She edged back watching the helicopter settle on Lundy's grassy helipad to the edge of the village. The pilot signalled it was safe to disembark from the aircraft telling his two passengers to secure any loose clothing and for them to remain within his line of sight, avoiding the tail rotor and to assume the crouching position as they moved clear.

'Charlie's down at the quay helping the SOCO team load their gear on the cruiser, ready I think, to leave tomorrow,' Charlotte said. 'He suggested we meet up in the Tavern for lunch. Is it okay if I join you Cliff?' she asked, thinking he appeared somewhat vacant.

'Sure.'

'What's wrong?' Charlotte said.

'In truth I expected a warmer welcome than that,' Cliff admitted with a hint of playfulness.

Beer hadn't considered his chuckle was that loud.

'What's so funny lad?'

'Oh, nothing Boss, nothing at all,' Beer said with more than a touch of mischief.

Charlotte winced, 'You guys have only been gone a few days,' she said trying to defuse what she took to be genuine dismay. 'I'll catch you in the Tavern later, okay?'

'If you say so,' replied Cliff almost grudgingly.

'It's good to see you two safely back in one piece,' Charlie contributed to the gathering. 'A lot's happened in the last few days.'

Not one of the four of them could disagree.

'The islanders have aired their concerns, SOCO have completed their investigations and as you say, Francesca's behind bars. I guess we'll head back on the cruiser tomorrow with the team Beer, and leave you Cliff, to clear up any loose ends.' Charlie smiled. 'Mind you,' he added, 'I can't help but wonder what might happen next?'

'I guess we'll never know what really did happen Sir?' Beer said.

'Maybe not Beer. I assume nothing of your training to date had prepared you for all of this? It's been quite a case that's for sure.'

Cliff joined in, 'I hope I've not put you off all this policing lark, Beer?"

'No Boss, but I don't know what's next.'

'Well, I guess he's up for fast tracking on to a degree course and promotion isn't that right Sarge?'

'I'd say so Cliff, his enthusiasm is commendable, perhaps it's been novel for you to experience Cliff.'

Cliff raised his eyes towards Beer and frowned.

'What about you, Boss? Where do you go from here?'

Cliff glanced sideways; the other two weren't sure whether he was contemplating his answer or looking to Charlotte for inspiration. The world weary detective shrugged.

'Firstly, to ensure my last 53 working days are free from any stress, then I'll sit back and enjoy my over-generous pension. Not that I haven't relished every minute of the chase, because in honesty I have enjoyed most of it, but I'm glad it's now more or less over.'

'One thing SOCO found,' Charlie cut in disturbing Cliff's flight of fancy.

'What's that?'

'A substance which they are taking back to the lab to analyse, perfectly innocent at first glance, but maybe not. A pot of paint.'

The others looked inquisitive, waiting for its significance to be revealed.

'It's one of Francesca's art paints, Scheele's Green I believe, a vivid emerald hue. They say it's very unusual to find in an artist's palette these days because it's highly toxic.'

'How toxic?' Cliff's inquisitive nature had been aroused.

'The technician tells me it has a reputation of having been responsible for killing several accomplished artists and was used in the sewers of Paris to kill rats. Containing arsenic, she tells me, it became known as the paint to die for.'

FORTY SIX

The human desire to be loved had almost completely passed Cliff by. It would be fair to say he had become so hardened that not only did he experience little fear or pain but also the love of life these days. He had become resolved to the idea that alone would be all he would ever be, but now…

She sat poised like some beauty he was seeing for the first time, seated on the sofa opposite him. Her bare legs were crossed, tanned like the rest of her. Charlotte's blue Levi skirt hugged her form as did the white shirt, part unbuttoned about her neck. This indomitable woman possessed all the qualities Cliff had been unacquainted with for so very long – patience, trust, intelligence and love. She shook her head and in a youthful gesture brushed all but a few strands of red hair from across her face.

'It's incredible how little time you have to spend with someone to have a pretty good idea who they really are.'

Cliff hardened at Charlotte's words.

'You're kidding, aren't you?'

She squeezed his arm and said, 'Only a bit,' and gave him a smile.

Cliff wasn't going to let that go. 'So, tell me, who am I?'

'Are you sure you want to know?'

'Yes.'

'Well in many respects you're inadequate.'

That certainly got things off to a flying start. Cliff baulked at Charlotte's initial assessment, readying himself for what was to follow.

'You were married, weren't you?'

'Yerr, why?'

'Did you love your wife?'

'Of course,' he doubted the purpose of her inane questions.

'Were you close?'

'Yes, in the beginning. Years ago now.'

'So why did she leave you?'

'Because she ran off with…,' Cliff floundered.

'I know but did you at least try to stop her?'

'Yes.'

'How hard?'

'What's your point?'

'You have a problem with relationships, with women. You walk a line and you walk it alone. Are you happier on your own?'

'I was but not now. Honestly, I don't think I am telling you something you don't already know.'

'What are you telling me?'

'Don't rush me, Charlotte.'

'Is that all you can say Cliff?'

He was silent.

'The reality is men need women more as they get older and women need men less.' Charlotte explained.

'Where did you get that idea from?'

'It's the truth. Women in many ways are stronger characters and we become more independent and freer in our later years and are trusted to take on the role of caring for others.'

He held her about the shoulders at arm's length, believing she would regard it as a natural indication of his affection.

'I've never felt like this before. I don't know what you feel but I know how I feel.' He watched her face for a response.

Holding back, she picked her words carefully.

'All good things come to an end.'

'They don't need to Charlotte,' he said trying to sound nonchalant but failing miserably. The moment reminded him of how he felt a long while ago, when he proposed.

'I need to listen to my heart more, not my head,' he said.

'You worried me back along,' she impressed.

Cliff looked at her confused.

'Your heart!' Charlotte exclaimed.

'Oh right. I'll get it checked out, I promise. So how do you feel about us?'

FORTY SEVEN

Clarence's funeral took place at Northam Cemetery, Bone Hill, Bideford. Morwenna's ailing financial circumstances resulted in the District Council of Torridge organising and paying for a simple affair. Only a handful attended the short chapel service; Cliff, Beer, Charlotte and Morwenna. None had appreciated it was the policy of the Local Authority not to advertise publicly funded committals. Morwenna had wanted her Clarence cremated but the police insisted on a burial. It had been organised for Beer to pick Morwenna up and run her home afterwards to Newquay, for which she was grateful, greeting Cliff as if he was an old family friend. The funeral boasted no flowers or limousines and Cliff decided it was the most unelaborate funeral he had ever had the pleasure to attend. Although a very basic service, it was conducted with dignity and respect and attempted to give Clarence a proper send off.

Morwenna was, understandably, in a fair old state, hardly managing to hold back her emotions. She had turned out in what can only be described as a tired, ill-fitting Sunday best. It was possible to imagine that at one time the outfit suited and fitted her but that was in the past, long before moth balls had taken up residence in her wardrobe.

That evening Charlotte and Cliff attended a concert by the Bournemouth Symphony Orchestra at the Queen's Theatre in Barnstaple. Classical music wasn't something Cliff would normally gravitate towards but Charlotte had been keen to take advantage of one of the few occasions when she could hear them. One item the orchestra played which struck a chord with her was Ravel's mournful 'Pavane for a Dead Princess.' Her concert programme described it as not a funeral lament, but more an evocation of a slow, stately dance that a little princess might have performed in a Spanish court.

For Charlotte, she just loved the beauty and sensitivity of the piece which stirred spirits and emotions deep within her. For Cliff who was clearly exhausted, he slept through nearly all of the concert, without a single snore, until that is, the finale, Elgar's 'Land of Hope and Glory,' that woke him up. Later that night, back at Cliff's cottage in Appledore, Cliff enjoyed a full night's sleep, while Charlotte struggled to settle in a small sofa bed which she was convinced had been designed only to sit on.

The next morning they were up with the lark, down at Bideford Quay, catching the ship back out to Lundy. Cliff was as bright as a button, whereas Charlotte felt completely shattered. She slept throughout the majority of the crossing only to be greeted, on docking, by a complaining Cliff moaning how unsociable she had been.

They had been on the island hardly any time when an urgent message came through for Cliff:
'I've scanned you an article which appeared in The Guardian on Wednesday last, maybe you've not picked it up Cliff, or got word yet. I am making further enquiries and will keep you updated if I learn anything new.
Regards, Andrew Maunder, The Journal'

'There are calls for an independent investigation into a series of suicides at Eastwood Park Women's Prison in Gloucester. After the death of another inmate the number of suicides in total this year is nine. The unprecedented inquiry follows the death last week of Grace Francesca Nancekivell, who is believed to have stolen drugs from the prison's healthcare unit and overdosed. Her death bore similarities to other recent deaths in the jail. She was being held in remand awaiting trial for double murder.

'A spokesperson from the Home Office said, 'We need to take a fresh look at the difficulties Eastwood Park faces. With the women's prison population accelerating by 20% over recent months we know Eastwood faces significant challenges of overcrowding and issues with the quality of the forty year old accommodation. An inspection in May this year highlighted inmates were at serious risk of suicide, self-harm and psychiatric disorders. We have begun making improvements by introducing proper mental screening and healthcare, along with drug treatment and support services. Clearly not soon enough in the case of Grace Nancekivell.

'The inquiry with its limited time frame, budget and narrow remit will unfortunately just scratch the surface

and not get to address the root problems according to the Prison's Press Officer.'

Cliff immediately requested through official channels a telephone conversation directly with the Governor of HMP Eastwood Park Prison.

'How can I help you Detective Cranford?'

'It's good of you to talk to me Sir,' Cliff began, 'I'm calling with regard to your prisoner, Grace Francesca Nancekivell.'

There was a brief silence over the phone. The Governor judiciously took the last inhale of his inferior cigar. This was instantly followed by an uncontrollable brief bout of coughing. He stubbed out the cigar then opened his mouth to speak.

'Now deceased,' the Governor said, 'a very sad and grave affair. I believe you were the arresting officer. I can only share with you my personal regret and that of my staff.'

'I understand,' Cliff said in an attempt to appease the old boy. 'I know you are responsible for the operation, management and welfare in the prison, so I would be grateful if you could share with me details around Grace's recent suicide.'

'You will, I am sure, be aware that I, and all in the Prison Service are under enormous pressures with overcrowding and significant staffing problems. It's truly a sad indictment on our prison's today.' The Governor paused. 'What I can do is let you talk with the officer in charge of her wing who was the last to see her alive.'

Within a matter of minutes Cliff was put through. After introductions he asked about Grace's state of mind prior to her death. The officer informed him she was perfectly fine in the morning when he had seen her, and spoken to her directly. In fact, he clearly recalled they had discussed how vivid green the sea was in the painting she was doing of the island where she had once lived. Cliff enquired if anything happened that day, out of the ordinary, to which the officer replied there was no such thing as an ordinary day in prison. He did mention she got a telephone call mid afternoon. When Cliff asked if he could remember anything about the call, the officer said not really. Only that it was a woman's voice and Grace was very disturbed afterwards. He had little opportunity to talk to her as he was about to go off duty at the end of his shift. She was found dead in her single cell at 5.52pm that same afternoon.

Cliff asked, 'Do you have a recording of the telephone call?'

'No!' the officer was definite.

'Do you have any idea who called?'

'Not really.'

'Any suspicions of who it might have been, or what it was about?'

'Normally most calls to prisoners are monitored but, in this instance, because the call was from Grace's legal adviser, it wasn't recorded.'

'Would you have checked the contact?'

'No, we are not obliged to check each and every caller. You must appreciate detective, with over two hundred prisoners, we can get scores of calls each and every day.'

Knowing Grace had opted not to have a legal adviser meant that there was a mystery caller out there, whose words had maybe had such an impact on Grace's mental state it caused her to commit suicide. In Cliff's mind, this changed everything.

When the dramatic news of Francesca's death reached the islanders, it only heightened each and everyone's bewilderment. The bells of the Cathedral in the Sea, St Helen's Church, rang out with the traditional peal of eight bells, bidding a farewell to Grace's departing soul, and from the top of the church tower, a large white and blue Lundy flag flapped in the biting wind.

FORTY EIGHT

The following few days passed uneventfully as Cliff prepared to leave Lundy for one last time and return to the mainland. In the old Nick, his desk was piled high with many a file stacked in his 'Pending' tray and the awful coffee was still just as awful. Mind you he welcomed the opportunity to get back into his own bed.

The distant sky was filled with ripples of translucent white altocumulus drifting high in the winter air. It signalled a change was on its way and a sense that winter was stretching far ahead like the endless sea.

From the departing Oldenburgh, Cliff could clearly see the stark white form of the South Light, and rising above it, The Castle. He visualised, high at the heart of the island, the small quaint cottage of Stoneycroft. Quiet, resting contentedly amid its well kept lawned garden and surrounded by crumbling stone walls where birds would take refuge, he could almost sense its peace and tranquillity now.

He turned and looked away. He'd seen more than enough death. A solitary gull flew high overhead towards the island. As Cliff watched the island sink into obscurity in the mist until it was no more than a shadow being swallowed by the steel grey sea, he reflected on all that had happened. Far off he could see the calm was giving way to another winter's storm. Before long the distant horizon would be as one with the huge sky. Cliff raised the collar of his overcoat, pulling it tightly about his neck. He turned his face away from the icy rain carried on the bitter wind.

'There's been too many victims on Lundy, yet the greatest victim has been the island itself.' Cliff put his arm about Charlotte's shoulders and brooded on her words. Far off a lonely fog horn boomed like some supernatural force across the troubled ocean.

EPILOGUE

Spring saw Lundy burst into life and curiously the appearance of a large bouquet of flowers laid on the rocks at Devil's Kitchen. Shirley Brückner was the first to discover the flowers whilst undertaking her usual morning walk with her retriever Max. Just as Shirley had been the one to stumble upon Clarence's body six months earlier, so it fell to her to be the first to come upon the blooms. It had been the fragrance of the flowers, carried on the early morning breeze, that had probably first attracted the hound. Not one person on Lundy knew who had put them there and no one on the ship recalled anyone sporting such a bouquet. The only words with the blooms were handwritten on a small white folded card; *'For my beloved Clarence.'*

It was about that time that a small fresh posy was left before Clarence's headstone, and every month thereafter. The accompanying message contained hardly the usual words of sympathy that one might expect, but simply said *'How I miss those wonderful precious times we shared*

*together each month. I will hold you in my heart forever
my beloved Clarence. All my love.'*

Had anyone else visited Clarence's grave and been bothered to read the tribute, then for them that would have delivered a strange twist to an already unusual series of incidents.

Cliff called Morwenna every three or four months, on the pretext to see how she was doing. A fall shortly after the funeral had left her with a fractured hip and various complications which had meant she was no longer mobile or able to leave the house. Morwenna was comforted to hear the grave was being maintained as she hadn't visited since the funeral and would no longer be able to.

Cliff reflected that, had they been unable to identify Clarence, someone out there might well be wondering why those precious monthly visits of his had come to a sudden end. Cliff realised that the identity of the person who had left flowers and messages at Clarence's grave was likely to remain a secret, as was the identity of Francesca's mystery telephone caller and, for that matter, exactly what did happen on the island.

Cliff could only speculate knowing that it made little difference now.

Colin J. Beazley was born in London and, having briefly lived in Hertfordshire, moved with his wife to Devon where they raised their four sons. His passion for writing gains inspiration from life and all its complexities, of which there are many, as he creates stories that carry the reader on journeys of discovery and suspense. In recent years he has divided his time between home and exploring the west of Scotland as well as Slovenia and its Eastern European neighbours.